"I'm good at what I do."

Cara's gaze skittered across his mouth, lingering. "I'm pretty aware of the breadth of your skill set."

Her voice had dropped, turning sultry, and Keith's body hardened in an instant. Yeah, he how hot their kisses had

"Are you flirting with

"Not in the slightest. and I took copious no what I learned."

She pivoted and walked away, leaving Keith standing alone by the pool. With a tropical storm on the horizon and a grand reopening combined with a bridal expo in two days, Cara was a distraction he could not afford to indulge.

* * *

Don't miss Cara's sister's story, another Newlywed Games book, in *From Fake to Forever*, also on sale this month from Harlequin Desire.

* * *

From Ex to Eternity
is part of the Newlywed Games duet:
Two wedding dress designers finally get their chance
to walk down the aisle!

* * *

If you're on Twitter,
tell us what you think of Harlequin Desire!
#harlequindesire

Dear Reader,

It's raining weddings at Harlequin! I'm a sucker for any kind of wedding, and I love the flowers, the dresses, the romance—all of it. Cara Chandler-Harris, my heroine, loves weddings, too, but unfortunately, she has to participate in them from afar as a wedding dress designer. Her own wedding fiasco gave her a good reason to avoid all things male and marriage, yet an invitation to a bridal expo in Turks and Caicos throws both in her lap when she meets up with the man who left her at the altar. Should she forgive him? Or just forget him?

Keith Mitchell is as alpha as they come, but he's secure enough in his masculinity that running a bridal expo doesn't faze him in the slightest. That's a real man!

I had a lot of fun writing this book because it combines so many of my favorite elements: a sun-drenched exotic beach locale, a reunion romance between two people who have a painful past to reconcile and a heroine who doesn't take her lumps lying down.

When you read *From Ex to Eternity*, you'll no doubt love Cara's wisecracking sister, Meredith. If you're dying to know what happened that weekend in Vegas, pick up Meredith's story. It's also available this month—no waiting!

I hope you enjoy reading both sisters' stories as much as I enjoyed writing them.

Kat Cantrell

FROM EX
TO ETERNITY

—

KAT CANTRELL

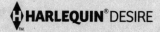
HARLEQUIN® DESIRE

Recycling programs
for this product may
not exist in your area.

ISBN-13: 978-0-373-73382-8

From Ex to Eternity

Copyright © 2015 by Kat Cantrell

Printed in U.S.A.

Kat Cantrell read her first Harlequin novel in third grade and has been scribbling in notebooks since she learned to spell. What else would she write but romance? She majored in literature, officially with the intent to teach, but somehow ended up buried in middle management in corporate America, until she became a stay-at-home mom and full-time writer.

Kat, her husband and their two boys live in north Texas. When she's not writing about characters on the journey to happily-ever-after, she can be found at a soccer game, watching the TV show *Friends* or listening to '80s music.

Kat was the 2011 Harlequin So You Think You Can Write winner and a 2012 RWA Golden Heart Award finalist for best unpublished series contemporary manuscript.

Books by Kat Cantrell

HARLEQUIN DESIRE

Marriage with Benefits
The Things She Says
The Baby Deal
Pregnant by Morning

Happily Ever After, Inc.

Matched to a Billionaire
Matched to a Prince
Matched to Her Rival

Newlywed Games

From Ex to Eternity
From Fake to Forever

Visit the Author Profile page
at Harlequin.com for more titles.

One

Even the sandpipers were getting more action than Cara Chandler-Harris.

But she was working at this Turks and Caicos resort instead of frolicking in the crystal-blue surf with a nearly naked, oiled companion. Cara would be the sole designer showcasing her fairy-tale-inspired wedding dresses to two hundred industry professionals at a three-day bridal expo. The wedding-dress fashion show was one of the premier events and Cara Chandler-Harris Designs, which was still in its fledging stages, was poised to explode with this once-in-a-lifetime opportunity for exposure.

Adding testicles into the mix would only drive her to drink.

Cara swept a glance over the woman in white silk standing before her in the Ariel wedding dress and repositioned the model to face forward. Wincing as she knelt for the four hundredth time, Cara stuck another pin through the lace-trim edging of the mermaid skirt.

"Don't forget her heels will be five inches. Not four," her assistant, and sister, Meredith, reminded Cara as she handed her another pin. "And yes, I checked with the airline again. The missing bag with the shoes in it will be here by four o'clock."

"Thanks, honey. I took her heel height into account. Is Cinderella ready to go?" Cara glanced at her sister.

Meredith nodded and flipped her long ponytail over her shoulder. "Won't need more than a slight waist alteration. I did good matching the models with the dresses, don't ya think?"

She had and knew it. Meredith wore her designer's assistant role like a second skin. Cara smiled. "Worried I'm going to fire you for ripping Aurora's sleeve?"

"Nah. I'm more worried about stuff I've done you don't know about yet." With a saucy, cryptic grin, Meredith handed Cara the final pin and hummed under her breath as she tapped out something on her phone.

"You know I hate that song," Cara mumbled around the pin in her mouth.

"That's why I sing it. If little sisters aren't annoying, what are we good for?"

"Herding the rest of the girls into place. We only have three days until the expo starts and we haven't even done one run-through." Her lungs already felt tight to be so far behind schedule. Good God Almighty. Missing luggage, torn dresses and a room with a faulty air conditioner. And it was only their first day in Grace Bay. "Why did I let you talk me into this?"

Cara had no idea how her name had come up to the powers that be who'd selected her for this event. Yes, a small handful of Houston brides had marched down the aisle in her dresses in the eighteen months she'd been in business, and yes, all of them had graced the pages of glossy society magazines. Yes, Chandler *and* Harris were both names everyone in Houston knew. But still. Grace Bay was a long way from Houston.

"Because you recognize my brilliance. Stop stressing. Plans can be altered."

"Dresses can be altered. Plans are carved in granite, and hell has a special level for those who mess with mine."

Meredith waved in two more visions in white who had appeared at the entrance to the pavilion, both barefoot, like the others. All of the models' shoes were in the missing bags.

"Where's Jackie?" Cara glanced back at the empty entrance.

"Puking her guts out," one of the girls responded with a ladylike shudder. "I told her not to drink the water."

Cara frowned. "The resort water is purified."

"Then something else is wrong with Jackie," Meredith said and rubbed Cara's shoulder. "A virus. It'll pass."

"It better. She has to be on stage in six days." A virus. Which could easily be transmitted to everyone else. Cara eyed Jackie's roommate. "How are you feeling, Holly?"

The willowy blonde in the French-lace concoction called Belle stared at Cara blankly. "It's not catching. Jackie's pregnant."

Now seemed like a really good time to sit down. Cara dropped onto the heavy tarp covering the sand, while the other girls squealed over Holly's announcement.

Meredith settled in next to Cara. "I didn't know. About Jackie. I would have—"

"It's not the end of the world. Women get pregnant. Women work while they're pregnant. All the time."

Her sister hesitated and then said, "I'll wear the dress for the run-through."

Thank God Meredith hadn't asked if Cara was okay. She'd had her fill of those kinds of questions two years ago, after her own pregnancy fiasco. Designing dresses had pulled her out of that misery and she didn't ever want to talk about it again.

"You can't wear it. The bust is too small and I can't alter it that much. Not here. Not in a few hours."

But the Asian-themed dress called Mulan wasn't too small for Cara.

The curse of average breasts.

Meredith had gotten Mama's gorgeous Chandler mahogany hair, the voluptuous Chandler body and the gracious Chandler mannerisms. Cara favored Harris blood, and Daddy was well-known for brains and business savvy, not his beauty. Neither Cara nor her father was dog-show worthy, but Cara certainly couldn't have claimed the Miss Texas crown like Mama and Meredith.

Cara staggered to her feet. "I'll wear it."

She'd worn it in the past. Not one dress with her name on the label escaped the Cara Test. When she finished the initial piece-together, she stood in front of the full-length mirror and said, "I do." If the words brought misty tears to her eyes, then the dress was right.

Except she always cried, because she created fantasies of lace and silk and happily-ever-after for someone else. Cara was just a glorified seamstress. A *single* seamstress.

She left Meredith and the chattering models in the pavilion and tottered through the sand to the concrete path leading into the heart of the resort. Twin five-story buildings lay on the outer perimeter and an enormous infinity pool dominated the space between. The pounding clamor of hammers rent the air, and scores of workers shouted to each other as they put the finishing touches on the renovations being executed for the resort reopening at the end of the week. The bridal expo was only a part of the festivities.

She skirted the pool, waited five minutes for the elevator, gave up and climbed the three flights of stairs to Jackie's room, near her own. Cara fetched the miserable girl some soda from the mini-fridge, then slipped into the dress flung haphazardly on Jackie's bed. Cara bit her lip and didn't say a word. Morning sickness sucked, and a dress that had taken Cara countless hours to envision and create likely rated pretty low on the list of Jackie's concerns.

The dress fit. Jogging, a low-carb diet and an extreme amount of willpower for everything except cabernet kept Cara's weight rock-steady. Cabernet calories didn't count.

The mirror taunted her but she didn't glance in it. Couldn't. Her reflection would only show what she already knew—she was always the bride, but never married.

Cara returned to the pavilion—barefoot, because her feet were already killing her and the broken elevator clearly hadn't been fixed yet despite the manager's promises. Cara had worn stilettos all day. Heels were as much a necessity as makeup and jewelry. A Chandler-Harris female did not leave the house unless fully dressed. But after the many problems she'd dealt with today, the last thing she wanted to do later was climb stairs in heels again.

She spent the next few minutes demonstrating to the girls how they should walk down the runway. To their credit, no one made a crack about how modeling was their job. If anyone had dared give Cara design instructions, she'd tell the person where to go, how fast and what to do upon arrival.

This was her life, her career, and nothing was going to keep her from replacing her dream of getting married with a flourishing wedding dress design business.

As Cara stood at the end of the runway going through a couple of more points, the girls shifted restlessly.

"Yummy," Holly whispered to Meredith, her eyes trained on something over Cara's shoulder. "That is one very well-put-together man."

Meredith's eyes widened to the size of salad plates. Cara spun, an admonishment on her lips designed to rid the pavilion of Yummy Interrupting Man. Whatever she'd been about to say died in her chest, and its death throes nearly coughed up her breakfast.

"Uh, Cara," Meredith whispered. "About that thing I did. The one you didn't know about… Surprise!"

Keith Mitchell, the devil in a dark suit, stood in the middle of her pavilion. He crossed his arms and cocked his head. His piercing gaze swept Cara from head to bare feet, lingering on the wedding dress. "Now, this looks familiar."

"Well, well, well. As I live and breathe." Cara fanned herself in mock Scarlett O'Hara style and did her best cat-with-a-canary smile. Stretching those particular muscles stung her face. "It's my very own runaway groom. Still got on your Speedy Gonzales shoes?"

Keith glanced at his fifteen-hundred-dollar Italian lace-ups. "They're functional."

"Lucky for you, sugar." She nodded. "There's the door. Use it."

He grinned, white teeth gleaming. "Sorry to disappoint you, honey, but I'm afraid this is my show."

"What show?" She waved at the wedding dresses and swallowed against the grapefruit in her throat. *Keith Mitchell.* What in the world was he doing in Grace Bay? "You're here to volunteer as my replacement model? I might have a dress in the back in your size."

Ha. Not even one of Keith's long legs would fit in a dress, and besides, he'd exited the womb wearing a suit. An unwrinkled suit because wrinkles did not dare to tread in his world.

Keith. Here in Grace Bay and standing five feet from Cara while she wore a *wedding dress.* Her bare toes curled in mortification. She was naked without her heels.

"Not the fashion show. The whole show." Keith winked, as only he could. "Regent Group hired me to turn this re-sort into the highest-rated wedding destination in the world.

If I do it right, I'll then have the opportunity to replicate it with their other Caribbean properties."

Oh, God. He was here to star in her very own personal nightmare and take up all the oxygen on the entire island while he was at it. "This is what you're doing now? Weddings? You aren't a particular fan of weddings, as I recall."

"This is the very best kind of wedding. No bride." He chuckled and nodded at Cara. "Or at least that was the intent when I took the job. I stand corrected."

Her blood, dormant for two long years, started pumping in her veins, flushing her face with heat she'd never let on was more than a becoming blush. Cara had generations of gracious Southern women in her DNA.

"I was invited to participate and I design wedding dresses. If you weren't aware, perhaps you need to find a job you're more qualified for," she said sweetly.

Meredith made a little noise in her throat at Cara's tone, likely in warning. Rattlesnakes had a tail. Most men never saw Cara coming.

Keith, who wasn't anything close to most men, just laughed. "I knew. But I wasn't expecting you to be wearing one. Brings back fond memories."

"Save it, Mitchell. What do I have to do to get you out of my way for the next six days?"

His lips pursed as he raked her with a smoldering once-over. With close-cut hair the color of a midnight sky, a body strenuously kept in prime condition and deep caramel eyes, he was unfortunately the very definition of six-foot-three-inches worth of yummy. Always had been.

"Oh no." She shook her head as her body hummed without her permission. "Get your mind out of the sheets. You could have slept with me all you wanted if you'd taken a short walk down the aisle. That barn door's closed to you. Forever."

All traces of yumminess went out the window as his face

hardened. Mitchell the Missile wasn't known for turning around failing companies because people liked his looks. Uncompromising, ruthless and detached—that was the man in front of her. Just like the last time she'd seen him—in her dressing room, forty-seven minutes before the flutist was scheduled to start playing *Canon in D*.

"We're going to be working together, Cara. Very closely. I suggest you get over our unfortunate history and be professional."

The models had gone quiet behind her, but every set of eyes burned into her back.

"Honey, I didn't have much to get over." That was a complete lie but she grinned through it. "I was over it five minutes after you left."

Also a lie. He didn't call her on it, though she was pretty sure he saw right through her.

"Then we have no problem. I'll buy you a drink later and we can catch up."

"As tempting as that sounds, I'll pass. Professionals don't drink on the job."

Keith left the beach pavilion with his head intact, a plus when unexpectedly confronted with an entire roomful of women in wedding dresses. God save him from brides.

He strode through the resort, noting a hundred issues requiring his attention. Tablet in hand, his admin, Alice, scurried after him, logging every sentence from his mouth in her efficient shorthand. She'd long grown accustomed to his ground-eating pace, and the ability to keep up was one of her many competencies.

He appreciated competency.

As he evaluated the construction crews' progress, checked in with the restaurant and catering staff and worked through a minor snafu with the recreation equipment, the image of Cara in that long white dress darted along the edges of his mind.

Not just in a dress, but in charge, running a business she'd created herself.

The harder he tried to forget, the more he thought about her. It was *Cara* but Cara unlike he'd ever seen her before. It was as oddly compelling as it was distracting.

That had not been his intent when he'd selected her for the bridal expo. Her connections were significant and her dresses had created consumer buzz in a tight industry, particularly among the moneyed crowd. Personal feelings couldn't interfere with what he knew this expo needed. Keith only had room for the best, and thorough research told him he'd found that in Cara Chandler-Harris Designs.

The decision to go with Cara was easy. Seeing her again was not.

Cara was a cold, scheming woman, no doubt. *All* women were scheming—or at least the ones he'd dated were—but Cara had proved to be the worst by trying to trap him into a marriage he didn't want. Thankfully, her scheme hadn't worked and he'd gotten out before it was too late.

He would never again make the mistake of agonizing over the decision to ask a woman to be his wife, only to find his effort was all for nothing. It had taken considerably longer than five minutes to get over it, but he'd moved on and rarely thought about his former fiancée…until today.

This consulting job had dominated his focus for the better part of six months. Regent Group had hired him to revive an anemic line of Caribbean resorts, and evidence of the life he'd pumped into this property's veins bustled around him. He thrived on insurmountable challenges.

Cara wasn't but a small, necessary cog in a larger machine and couldn't become a further distraction, no matter how much of a surprise it was to discover he was still dangerously attracted to her.

"Alice, please send a bottle of cabernet to Miss Chandler-Harris's room. Cara," he clarified as he and Alice evaluated the pool area. Meredith drank martinis, with two olives. Obviously quite a few things with the sisters had changed, but not that, he'd bet.

"Yes, sir," Alice responded.

The largest infinity pool in the Caribbean spread out between the two main buildings. The pool's dark basin turned the water a restive navy in deliberate contrast to the turquoise ocean. Intimate concrete islands dotted the outer edge of the pool and would be set up for private dining later in the week.

A breeze picked up strength and rattled the multicolored umbrellas in their stands. Half the stands were empty, yet another in the long list of issues. Many of the thousands of resort projects he'd meticulously approved for implementation had already been done, but not enough. The work teams should be much further along.

Now that he'd arrived, his firm hand would guide the teams into executing the strategy or he'd guide the offenders into the unemployment line.

Keith Mitchell did not allow others to fail on his watch.

In three days, the grand reopening would coincide with a three-day bridal expo. Dozens of merchants, media executives and other wedding professionals composed the elite group of people invited for the resort's relaunch as a premier wedding destination.

Cara's fashion show was one of the highlights of the party.

The image of Cara in a wedding dress continued to compete for his attention. Those bare feet peeking out from under the hem had done a quick, sharp number on his lower half. He'd only ever seen her out of heels when she'd been out of everything else, as well. Naked Cara was a sight worthy of recalling.

They'd had chemistry to spare two years ago, and it hadn't fizzled in the least. A slight miscalculation on his part, but manageable.

The resort manager met him in the lobby, dead center over the inlaid Carrera marble Regent emblem. Elena Moore took his hand in her firm grip. "Mr. Mitchell, welcome back. I'm pleased to see you again."

"Likewise." He'd hired Elena personally and their management styles meshed well. "Show me what you've accomplished."

His last visit had been three weeks ago, and Elena's staffing efforts had dramatically improved since then. Nearly all of the openings in the organizational chart now listed names, and most had received training. They discussed Elena's biggest hurdles until Keith was satisfied with their agreed direction.

Elena showed him to the two-bedroom penthouse suite he'd requested and disappeared. Two pieces of matched luggage bearing Keith's initials sat inside the room, though they hadn't passed the porter. Invisibility—the mark of excellent hotel service. Keith had earned his road-warrior status traveling as many as three hundred days a year, and if he knew anything, it was hotels.

Everything in his life was temporary by design because soon enough, he'd be moving on to the next job. He preferred it that way.

The seventeen-hundred-square-foot suite had been equipped with three flat-screen TVs, a kitchenette and wireless internet connectivity, precisely according to Keith's specifications. When the resort reopened, guests in this suite would have the services of a dedicated concierge, as well.

He tested everything twice. Satisfied, Keith unpacked his clothes and hung his suits in the walk-in closet, taking up only one of the four available racks. He traveled light and alone, always, but guests would appreciate the space.

After calling down to room service for someone to iron his shirts, he washed away the airplane stench in the enormous glass-enclosed shower. Work beckoned but he took a much-needed fifteen-minute break with a frosty Belgian white from the mini-fridge—his preferred type of beer. The staff knew his preferences, as they should and would know the same about every guest in this hotel.

He settled into a solitary chair outside and took a long pull from the bottle. The wraparound terrace offered a 180-degree view of the pristine shoreline, tinted light pink in the dying rays of the sunset. It was a slice of perfection, and those who wished to tie the knot with such unparalleled beauty surrounding them would pay handsomely because every hand-selected staff member paid attention to details.

Keith Mitchell always hit his target.

He worked until his eyes crossed, then slept a solid four hours and rose at dawn to go jogging. He'd barely finished stretching when another early riser came onto the beach a hundred yards down the shore. Normally, he'd give other people a wide berth, as he always opted to be alone whenever he could. It was the nature of consulting to be constantly on the move. Lasting attachments made zero sense and he was typically too busy to get sentimental about the lack of relationships in his life.

But his Y chromosome had absolutely no trouble recognizing Cara, and their brief exchange yesterday hadn't satisfied his curiosity about what she'd done with her life over the past two years. And he had a perverse need to understand why she still got under his skin after all the lies she'd told him.

Keith caught up with her. "When did you start jogging?"

She shot him a sidelong glance. "I might ask you the same question."

He shrugged. "A while back. Not getting any younger."

"Who is?" She threaded brown hair through a ponytail holder and raised her arms in a T, swiveling at the waist. Her red tank top stretched across her torso and rode up to reveal a smooth expanse of flesh. New blond streaks in her hair gleamed against the backdrop of ocean. "Which way are you going?"

He jerked his head to the left and tore his eyes off Cara's body. Reluctantly. "Interested in joining me?"

"No." She curled her lip. "I'm interested in heading the opposite direction."

"Careful. You wouldn't want anyone to get the wrong idea. That sounded an awful lot like someone who isn't over me yet."

"Get your hearing checked."

But she took off in the direction he'd planned to go, face trained straight ahead. He matched her stride and they ran in silence about three feet from the rushing surf. Not companionable silence. Too much unsaid seethed between them for friendliness, faked or otherwise.

The September weather was perfect, still cool in the morning, and later, Grace Bay would hit the mideighties. The first time Keith set foot on Regent's Turks and Caicos resort, he'd immediately designated it the centerpiece of the corporate-wide luxury-wedding-destination renovation. No one would be disappointed with the choice.

After half a mile or so, he expected Cara to peel off or fall to the sand, gasping for air. She kept going, stretching it out to a mile. Impressive. She wasn't even winded. The Cara he'd known had balked at anything more strenuous than painting her nails.

But then, he hadn't really known her at all.

By mutual agreement, they turned around to head back to the resort. At the entrance marker to the private beach, they slowed and then stopped.

Cara walked in circles to cool down and Keith watched her on the sly as he peeled his damp shirt from his chest to wipe his forehead. Her skin had taken on a glow and she'd yet to slather her face with half a cosmetic store. Dressed-to-the-nines Cara he liked, especially when he took her to dinner and got to spend a whole meal fantasizing about stripping her out of all that finery.

This natural version of her hit him with a sledgehammer to the backs of his knees.

No distractions, Mitchell.

Yet, Cara had never stuck to the role he'd assigned her in his life. Why had he been daft enough to believe that might have changed?

She noticed him watching her and crossed her arms over a still-heaving chest. "Tell me one thing. Why me? Out of all the wedding dress designers out there."

"Your name was on the short list. Much to my shock."

"Is it that difficult to believe I can sew?" Her chin jutted out, daring him to say yes.

But it *was* inconceivable that she'd traded a burning desire to trap some clueless male into marrying her for a design business.

"You have a degree in marketing. Two years ago, you were a junior coffeemaker at an ad agency and then, *bang*. Now you're Cara Chandler-Harris Designs, so pardon my mild cardiac arrest. Despite that, your name is highly respected in the industry and I need the best. That's why you made the cut."

Plus, he was curious to find out if she was merely the face of the company. Maybe she had someone else slaving away over the dresses while she took all the credit.

"For your information, *bang* took eighteen months of sleepless nights and several design classes to accomplish. I got an interest-bearing loan. No one handed me anything."

Not even her father? Seemed unlikely that John Harris would have done *nothing* to help his daughter's business.

"Doesn't hurt to have Chandler-Harris on the label either."

"It's not a crime to have connections. If memory serves, the president of Regent Group's board is married to a friend of my mom's. Tell me it's a coincidence you're now working for Regent."

Her gaze sliced into him and he didn't dare grin. But he wanted to. She'd never had so much attitude. He liked it. "All successful people have connections."

"Exactly. And I'm going to continue using mine." The dawn light beamed across her face and caught a wicked glint in her espresso-colored eyes.

Keith filed that fact away—for later, when he might lean on their connection. Though he had no doubt she intended to use her connection to him in an entirely different way than he did. "But wedding dresses?"

"Funny story. I got left at the altar and had this useless dress I'd made myself."

A flash of memory surfaced—Cara in a white dress with hundreds of beads sewn to the top and a stricken look on her face when she turned to see him at the door of her dressing room. He'd stayed long enough to discover the truth about his fiancée. And then left.

"You made that dress?"

With a withering glare, she plopped down in the sand and pulled on a flexed foot. "If you'd paid attention during the wedding plans, that wouldn't be new information."

"If you'd been reasonable about the plans, I might have paid more attention." She'd been like bridezilla on steroids.

"It was my *wedding*, Keith." She closed her eyes for a beat and muttered under her breath. All he caught was the word *professional*.

It had been his wedding, too, a fact she seemed to have

forgotten, but in reality, he hadn't cared about the center-pieces or the color of the cake. He'd given her free rein. Gladly, and then tuned it all out. A wedding was an event to be endured. Much like the marriage he didn't ask for but agreed to because it was the right thing to do.

"So, you made the dress yourself. Then what happened?"

She glanced up at him, her expression composed. "Norah asked me if I could alter it to fit her. So I did and she wore it when she got married later that month. Then Lynn asked me if I could make one for her. I have yet to run out of un-married sorority sisters and friends, so a design business was born."

Norah and Lynn. Bridesmaids number three and four. He had a healthy bit of distance from Houston now, and per-spective on his almost-marriage, but he'd been unprepared for it to feel like weakness to recall details with such clarity.

He should go back to his room and shower. Opening day loomed and nothing productive could come of continuing this conversation. "Do you like it?"

Surprise flitted across her face as she climbed to her feet, pointedly ignoring his outstretched hand. "I do. It wasn't what I envisioned for myself, but I needed…" She took a breath and he had the impression she'd changed her mind about what she'd been about to say. "It was something to occupy my time."

Finally, something that made sense. The design busi-ness was a time killer for an aspiring trophy wife obsessed with finding a husband she'd been unable to snag thus far. Every woman Keith had ever dated wanted nothing more than a free ride and the prestige of being Mrs. Mitchell. Cara was no different.

Except for the part where she started her own business. It was as perplexing as it was fascinating. And he had the feeling she'd been telling the truth when she claimed to have done it with no help from her rich daddy. Keith was thoroughly impressed, quite against his will.

"You come highly regarded for something you fell into accidentally."

"I prefer to think of it as providence."

"So you'd design one-use-only dresses no matter what? Why not something more practical?"

"Ever made a cake?"

"I've eaten cake. Does that count?"

Her eyes rolled. "Sometimes when you bake a cake, it doesn't cook quite right. Maybe it's lopsided or part of it sticks to the pan. Frosting covers a multitude of baking sins. A wedding dress is like frosting. My brides feel beautiful, even if they don't feel that way wearing anything else. I'm responsible for that, and it's amazing."

Frosting was one-use-only, too. Had she chosen the analogy purposefully? "You *are* using your marketing degree, then. It's all false advertising in the end."

False advertising. Her best skill.

"Lord have mercy on your cynical soul." She jumped up and brushed sand from the backside of her formfitting jogging pants. No one could fault a man's eyes for straying to the nicely rounded area under her fingers. "One wonders why you asked me to marry you in the first place."

He snapped his focus away from her curves. Her frosting hid a multitude of sins, as well. "Because you were pregnant."

Or so she'd led him to believe.

Two

Cara escaped before she actually sank down into the white sand for a good cry. She slammed the door to the room she shared with Meredith. Hard. Hopefully, her devious sister was still sound asleep. "How could you do this to me?"

The blanket on Meredith's bed moved slightly and incoherent speech rumbled from beneath it.

"Was that English?" Cara ripped the blanket off the bed. "It's like ninety degrees in here. How can you sleep under this?"

Meredith peered up at Cara through slitted eyes. "Which question do you want me to answer? Without a cup of coffee in my hand, you only get one."

"Keith. You knew he was behind the invite." Several people had casually dropped information about his new consulting gig into conversations, but she'd been too busy ignoring anyone who mentioned Keith's name to realize Regent owned this resort.

"Sue me. You needed this expo deal to grow your business. Where's the harm?" Flipping hair out of her face, Meredith sat up, looking as if she'd just rolled out of a lingerie fashion shoot instead of bed. If Cara didn't love her sister so much, she'd hate her. "He's just an ex-fiancé. A guy you are completely over. Right?"

"Totally." *Well, mostly.*

Cara sank onto the bed and brooded. She needed a shower and a sturdy wooden stake to drive through the heart of the walking corpse masquerading as a man named Keith Mitchell.

"Don't protest too hard or you'll hurt yourself. If nothing else, it's a chance for closure. Take it." Meredith's gaze grew keen. "You were fine with this yesterday. What happened?"

"Keith jogs now. Or did you already know that, too?"

Meredith stuck her tongue out. "You two are made for each other. Only insane people get up at the crack of dawn to *run*. Clearly he's lost as many marbles as you have."

"Oh, he's still in possession of all his faculties. What he's lost is his humanity."

"Because he's giving you exclusive worldwide exposure for your dresses? You're right, that's way over the line."

Cara buried her face in her hands and dredged up some Magnolia Grit. She had it to spare or she'd never have made it out of her wedding-day dressing room after losing not one, but two of the most important things in her life. Now would be a great time for that grit to surface. "He only asked me to marry him because I told him I was pregnant. How did I not know that?"

"A lot of guys wouldn't have. He did." Meredith's arms wrapped around Cara and the silent unconditional support nearly undid her. "Still, it's a crappy thing to admit. Even if it's true."

With a sniffle, Cara nodded against Meredith's shoulder. "I thought he loved me."

"One is not mutually exclusive of the other. He probably did love you. Maybe he was going to ask you at some point in the future and you gave him an incentive to speed up the timing."

"Yeah and that worked out."

"Better you found out then that he's a rolling stone. I was never fond of the name Cara Chandler-Harris Mitchell anyway. If you guys kiss and make up, consider keeping your maiden name this time."

She scowled. "I'd rather kiss the hind end of a sweaty camel than Keith."

The knowing smile Meredith shot over her shoulder on her way to hog the bathroom did not improve Cara's mood. "I could've lit the candles on a ninety-year-old's birthday cake from all the sparks shooting around the pavilion yesterday."

"That was Keith's robotic heart short-circuiting."

"You might be over him, but that man is definitely not over you. People make mistakes. Maybe he wants another chance."

"Another chance to crush me beneath him as he rolls away again? Ha."

Lord Almighty. Now she was replaying their conversations through her head. This morning on the beach, he'd been genuinely curious about her life. And okay, he always radiated that carnal come-hither, but more of it had wafted in her direction than she'd been willing to acknowledge.

"Honey, you're a smart girl. Do the math." Meredith leaned on the bathroom door frame. "He didn't invite you here solely for your fantastic wedding dresses. Hell, I can slap some lace on a piece of satin and stick it on some starry-eyed bride. He wants the designer. Not the designs."

"He can want until all the gears in his robotic heart rust. I have a brand-new lease on life and no man, especially not Keith Mitchell, is a part of the plan." Cara elbowed past

Meredith into the bathroom. "And for the crack about slapping lace on satin, you forfeit first dibs on the shower."

Grumbling, Meredith conceded and shut the door behind her. Cara fumed as she stood under the jets.

So. The invitation was a veiled attempt to reconcile, was it? Shattered pieces of her life and her heart had taken a supreme amount of will to recover. There was no way on God's green earth she'd consider forgiving Keith for walking out on her when she'd needed him most.

He was not husband material. Period.

She dressed for the day in her best heels and a flattering outfit—the modern-day woman's equivalent to a full suit of armor.

As the Good Lord clearly felt she deserved a break, the elevator button lit up when she pressed it. A working elevator. About time.

Then the doors slid open to reveal the very man she least wanted to see.

Keith smiled and sizzled her toes with a heated glance at her Louboutin sandals. "Going down?"

"You first." She waltzed in to stand right next to him because she was a professional. An elevator full of testosterone didn't scare her. The idea Meredith had planted—about how Mr. Runaway Groom might be angling for a do-over—*that* put a curl of panic in the pit of her stomach.

Why, she didn't know. There wasn't a combination of words in any language he could utter that would make her crazy enough to try again. And to the best of her knowledge, Keith was fluent in five languages and could order beer in twelve more.

She stared at the crack where the two door panels met and pretended the tension hadn't raised the hair on her arms. Keith's heat instantly spread through the small box and started seeping through her pores. And she'd already been plenty hot and bothered. He was just so solid and powerful and...*arrogant*.

"Do you run every day?" Keith asked politely.

"Usually. You?" Oh, her mama would be so proud. Twenty-eight years of lessons on how to smile through the Apocalypse were paying off.

"I try to. It's great for clearing my head."

Cara bit back her first response—*Is that what happened to your brain when you cooked up the idea of a second chance?* "Oh?"

"It's an opportunity to hone my focus for the day ahead."

"Sorry I intruded this morning."

Keith glanced at her but she didn't take her eyes off the crack. "You didn't. I enjoyed it."

All this civility slicked the back of her throat. Why was it taking so long to reach the ground floor? The building was only five stories.

The elevator screeched to a halt, throwing Cara to her knees. Before she hit the carpet, the interior went black.

Of course. It wasn't enough to be on a small island with Keith. Now they were trapped in an elevator together. In the dark.

"Are you okay?" Keith's voice split the darkness from above her. Obviously he had superior balance in his flat shoes.

She eased back against the wall, wincing as her ankle started to ache. Twisted, no doubt. "Fine."

A glow emanated from Keith's hand. "Flashlight app."

"Do you have a call-the-elevator-repairman app? That would be handy."

"I'm texting the hotel manager as we speak." He sank to the floor and leaned against the back wall, crossing his mile of legs gracefully. "At least there's no chance we'll plunge to our deaths. I think we're stuck between the second and first floors."

"Can we climb out the hatch through the top?"

Keith set his phone on the floor and glanced at the ceiling. "Maybe. I'd have to boost you up. Could you pry the doors apart on the second floor?"

"On second thought, let's see how long it'll take the manager to get someone here to fix it. The temperature in here is cooler than my room. So there's that."

"What's wrong with your room?"

"Air conditioner is flaky."

In the low glow of the phone, Keith's frown was slightly menacing. "Why didn't you report it to the manager?"

"Oh, is *that* what you're supposed to do?" She pulled the sandal off her foot and massaged the offending ankle. Still hurt as if she'd stabbed it with a pair of shears. Well, if nothing else, now she had a good excuse to avoid jogging on the beach with a man who moved so fluidly it made her salivate. "I assume the manager called the same guy to repair it as the one who fixed the elevator. You'd think the consultant responsible for the whole show might have a better handle on this sort of thing."

"My shows always go off without a hitch. Did you hurt yourself?"

"I'm fine."

His phone beeped and he picked it up to tap through the message. "It'll be about twenty minutes. Can you live with that or shall we try the escape hatch?"

Twenty minutes in the close confines of an elevator with her ex-fiancé. If he tried anything, she'd stab him with her heel. There was wood in a stiletto, wasn't there? "I'll wait. I didn't have anything to do today besides lounge around at the pool."

"Me either."

She rolled her eyes. "Yeah, I know. You're the big man on campus. How come you're not CEO of something by now? Too permanent?"

His sculpted lips pursed, and dang it if it didn't set off a flutter to recall how masterfully that mouth could pleasure her body. The curse of celibacy. Her neglected body needed to catch a clue about how totally unattractive Keith Mitchell was.

Well, not on the outside, but on the inside, where it counted.

"I have no desire to be the CEO of anything," he said. "I'm my own boss. I can pick my challenges and move on, instead of being mired in entrenched bureaucracy at a company long-term."

Yep. Meredith had called it. At least Cara had found out about his allergy to commitment before she'd married him. But now she had a ton of other questions.

She should shut up. Being stuck in an elevator didn't mean she had to say everything on her mind. "Just for morbid grins, once we'd gotten married, how long would it have taken you to develop the seven-year itch—six months?"

So apparently she *did* have to hash it out right this minute.

His crisp suit rustled as he shifted into a different position. "I let it go earlier, but let's clear this up now. I didn't leave you at the altar. I'm sure it's more fun to tell the story that way. Gets you a lot more sympathy."

She laughed but it rang hollow. "Semantics, Mitchell."

"It's not. I wouldn't have subjected you to the public humiliation of walking down the aisle to an empty spot where I was supposed to be."

"Well, bless your heart. I really appreciate you sparing me the humiliation of having to call off my wedding minutes before it started. Oh, wait. That *is* what happened. Fill me in on the part where you were acting noble."

If this was a reconciliation attempt, he should stick to his non-long-term day job.

"Cara." He heaved a sigh. "Timing aside, we weren't

meant to be. Our marriage would have been a disaster. Surely you've come to accept that during the last two years."

"That was a lame excuse then and time hasn't improved it. I needed you and you left."

"You needed a wedding and a husband. Anyone with the proper equipment would've done. It just took me a while longer to wise up than it should have."

"I was in love with you!" She curled her hand into a fist and imagined planting it right in his arrogant jaw. A girl could dream. Probably it would break her hand before it rearranged his pretty face.

"Right." He smirked. "Just like I was in love with you."

He didn't believe her.

All vestiges of Southern grace evaporated as a snarl escaped her clamped lips. "Unlike you, I wasn't getting married because of the baby. I was deluded enough to believe we were going to be a happy family."

"That mythical happy family would have been a little difficult considering you lied about being pregnant."

"What?" She shook her head but the roaring in her ears just swelled. "I didn't lie about being pregnant."

"You flashed a fake smile and said, 'Guess what? False alarm.' Convenient how you discovered it moments before the ceremony. That's the reason I spared you the walk down the aisle, because you told me before instead of after."

"False al—" She recoiled so hard, the back of her head smacked the wall. "I had a miscarriage, you son of a bitch."

"A miscarriage?" Keith's pulse stumbled and his lungs contracted. "How is that possible?"

"You've heard of the internet? Do a search." Cara crossed her arms and looked away, but not before he caught the tremble of her lower lip in the phone's glow.

That punched him in the gut. "On what planet does

'false alarm' mean a miscarriage instead of 'not really pregnant'?"

The harsh tone had come out automatically. If he couldn't keep better control over himself, he might check out the escape hatch regardless, which would be very difficult to maneuver with his foot in his mouth. But if she'd really been pregnant, everything he'd assumed about her, about their relationship—hell, maybe even about himself—was wrong.

"Planet Bride-Dealing-With-Whacked-Out-Hormones. It's in the I-Get-A-Pass Galaxy. I didn't want to ruin our special day with something so awful." She muttered "Jerk" under her breath, but she didn't cry.

It was a far tamer slur than the one he was calling himself. Miscarriage. He still couldn't wrap his head around it. "You were really pregnant?"

"Guess you get to keep your genius status one more day."

He was so far from a genius, he couldn't even see the "stupid" line he'd crossed. His temples throbbed with tension and unrestrained nerves.

Miscarriage was the false alarm.

From the moment Cara told him about the pregnancy, he'd been so furious, with himself for not being more diligent about birth control, with how difficult it had been to come to terms with what needed to happen next—regardless of his intense desire to avoid matrimony—and with Cara's happiness over a marriage he didn't want.

Meredith had found him nursing his wounds the morning of the wedding and announced, "Cara needs to talk to you," with such gravity.

He'd fallen on the words "false alarm" like a starving dog on a steak, and as a bonus, he assumed Cara had created a manipulation scheme. Then he'd settled into his role of martyr with ease.

He rubbed his eyes but it only made the sting worse and didn't change what his vision had already told him—

she was telling the truth. "At what point were you going to clarify this?"

"After the ceremony, when we were alone. Figured we could cry about it together and drown our sorrows in expensive champagne I could actually drink." She cocked her head and the heat of her anger zinged through the elevator. "You thought I'd lied about being pregnant? How in all that's holy can you believe I would do something so reprehensible?"

Keith ran a hand across the back of his clammy neck. This conversation was veering into a realm he did not care for. "How could you believe I'd walk out on you if I'd really understood what you meant? Why didn't you stop me?"

Smooth. If she'd just give him a minute to collect his scattered wits, he might formulate a response that didn't make him sound like a callous ass.

I'm so, so sorry. I should have asked more questions. I screwed up.

As always, he could no sooner force such emotionally laden words out of his mouth than he could force a watermelon into it.

"Because I knew, Keith! I could see the relief dripping from your expression. You never invested an ounce of effort into the wedding plans and I blew it off as typical guy hatred of flowers and musical selections. But you stood there, all calm and cool, telling me how we wouldn't have worked out anyway. Miscarriage or false positive, it's the same end. You were looking for an out and I handed it to you."

You're right. I was.

The exit had been calling his name before she'd dropped the pregnancy bomb that then tightened the noose with alarming haste. His first love was a job well done, completed by the sweat of his brow. He'd been fortunate his hard work over the years had resulted in a healthy bank account. Women typically wanted a piece of it. Providing a lavish lifestyle for an unambitious wife who wanted nothing more than to spend his money put Keith off the idea of tying himself permanently to any of them. Only an unexpected pregnancy could have turned the tide.

Of course he'd jumped to the wrong conclusion. Of course he didn't hang around to dissect it. Those dominoes had been set up long before that final showdown. Maybe even as far back as childhood, when he'd watched his mother come home with Bergdorf bags three times a week and trade in her Bentley once a year.

It didn't make him feel any better about what he'd done. "I'm... I... You didn't deserve that."

There was more he should say, but it stalled in his throat. For once in his life, he had no idea how to handle a situation. No idea what to do with the clawing, suffocating guilt lodged in his windpipe.

Keith Mitchell was never caught off guard. Never at a loss for words.

"No, I didn't deserve any of it. But I'm glad it went down like it did. Otherwise we'd be divorced by now."

"That's low. I would have stayed with you for the sake of the baby."

Just as he'd intended to marry her for the sake of the baby. He'd hoped he and Cara might eventually become friendly, like his parents, and have an amicable marriage. She had connections and would be good for his public image, a tradeoff for giving her his name. It was an uneven compromise but one he'd been willing to make.

The baby part of the equation, he did not want to think about. He wasn't cut out to be a father. Despite all the pain, it had worked out for the best.

"I wouldn't have stayed with *you*. That's not the marriage I wanted." She sighed. "I'll probably shoot myself later, but I'm about to agree with you. We wouldn't have worked out. You're a crap-head of the first order, but you did me a favor by leaving. Meredith was right. I needed closure and now I've got it."

The knot in his larynx cinched a notch. Where had this woman *come* from? The Cara of two years ago was a completely different person than the one slouched against the elevator sidewall.

Before, she'd been flirty and fun, someone to spend time with until things ran their course or he moved on to the next job in the next city. He'd never seen their relationship as progressing toward anything serious. When she'd announced the pregnancy, the decision to marry her had come about slowly and painfully. But it took two to tango and Keith never reneged on his responsibilities.

This present-day Cara had an enigmatic blend of strength, wit, drive and determination.

And it was stunning on her.

He cleared his throat. "You said you were in love with me. Is that true?"

She'd never said that before, not even in the weeks before the wedding.

"I thought I was. Now I'm not so sure." She shook her head. "All this time you thought I wasn't actually pregnant? Lord, the names I called you for walking away from a woman who'd just had a miscarriage. Mama would have made me wash my mouth out with soap if she'd heard me."

He cleared his throat. It didn't help shake free the phrase he couldn't withhold any longer. "Cara, I… I'm…sorry. What can I do?"

"You made a mistake and you apologized. It's enough."

"Not for me."

"Sorry, Keith. You don't get to decide. I've already forgiven you."

Her casually tossed-out sentiment blazed past the knot and spread warmth through his frozen chest. Forgiveness. Freely offered. It was a gift he'd never been given, never solicited. Never wanted. Now that he had something so significant…what did he do with it?

She rolled her shoulders. "Now maybe this week won't be as gruesome as I've envisioned."

The overhead lights flickered, then shone steadily, and the elevator lurched. The doors slid open on the ground floor and Cara slipped on her shoe, then climbed to her feet, flinching as her left foot hit the marble in the lobby.

Keith snagged her hand before she could bolt. "Are you going to be able to walk on that ankle?"

Lean on me. I won't let you down this time.

"It's still attached, isn't it? Nothing a good bottle of wine won't cure."

"Let me bring you one. Later tonight."

More questions about the past rose up, struggling to be voiced, such as how it had happened, when she'd gone to the doctor. He wasn't ready to let her go, but neither could he stutter through such an emotional maze. Not now. Later, after he'd processed, his coherency would surely return.

Those espresso-colored eyes danced down to their linked hands and back up again, skewering him. Her intense gaze was full of that mystique he'd begun to suspect had far more depth than anyone realized. Least of all him.

"I'm about Keith Mitchell-ed out for the day. When I said this week won't be as gruesome as I thought, I meant I could dismiss you from my mind without a scrap of remorse."

She slid from his grasp and hobbled across the lobby in pursuit of a goal that had nothing to do with Keith. And shouldn't.

But he'd never been very tolerant of being dismissed, especially not when in the company of a completely different Cara than he remembered. Her business, as best he could tell, was legitimate and indeed the product of a strong work ethic, which he thoroughly respected. Was it possible she wasn't just after a husband any longer? What could have prompted such a big turnaround?

This week had just gotten a whole lot more interesting.

Keith didn't see Cara again until after lunch, when Marla Collins, the expo event coordinator, called a meeting with all the participants. He leaned against a lone table along the back wall of the resort conference room and listened to the spiel from a distance. Alice sat in the first row typing up the highlights, which she would email to him afterward, but he preferred to hear the details firsthand.

His gaze strayed through the seated crowd to Cara's streaked brown hair as she leaned to whisper something in Meredith's ear. Telling her sister about Keith's evils, no doubt. Though she'd probably been doing that for two long years. Cara ran a business now. They likely had more pressing matters to discuss besides the callous ass in the back of the room.

Could she really have forgiven him so easily, in a scant few minutes?

He most assuredly had a hundred more pressing matters to occupy him, and yet the conversation in the elevator this morning never fully left his thoughts. How could it? For two years, he'd been convinced Cara had tried to trap him into a marriage he didn't want.

He'd moved on and had never lost sleep over it. Cara's expo invite was strictly intended to secure the best wedding industry professionals, not expose him to a newly altered reality. And in that mirror, he did not like his reflection. He'd hurt her. Keith Mitchell did not make mistakes.

Marla wrapped up the status meeting and the participants gathered their handouts and electronic devices, chattering to each other as they swarmed from the room. Keith waited for Cara to pass him and invented an excuse to speak to her, but no less than four people lined up to ask him questions or report a problem. He watched her leave with Meredith, never once glancing in his direction. Clearly, she meant to do exactly as she said—dismiss him from her mind. He wished he could do the same so easily.

This brand-new Cara intrigued the hell out of him. He couldn't let things lie between them, not with all her revelations. Not with those bare feet still lingering in his mind's eye. If nothing else, the ledger in his head needed reconciling. While she'd gotten her closure, he hadn't.

"Excuse me," he said to Elisabeth DeBolt, the manager of spa services, who had been midsentence in detailing the color of tile she'd selected for the massage rooms. Details he normally encouraged. But not right now.

He left Elisabeth and the others where they stood and followed Cara out the door.

Cara and Meredith hadn't gone far. They were near the pool, embroiled in what looked to be a fascinating conversation with a maintenance worker's pecs, which the two women's eyes never left. The shirtless pool boy blathered on to the sisters as if he didn't notice, likely used to being ogled by the ladies.

Keith made a mental note to have a word with the recreation manager. This resort would cater to couples, not singles. Shirtless pool boys with the ability to bench-press the equivalent of twice their own weight had their place but not at this property.

As Keith could also bench-press the equivalent of twice his own weight and topped the kid by five inches, Shirtless Pool Boy wisely took off when Keith joined their party.

"Thanks a whole heap, Mitchell. I was enjoying the view," Meredith grumbled. "No matter how good you look in a suit, I can't fantasize about you."

He grinned, his mood considerably lightened. He'd smiled more in the past two days than he had in the past two months. "Why not? Sister code?"

"No, because you're a cretin." She tossed her hair. "Unlike some other people I could mention, I don't forgive so easily. Keep that in mind next time you find yourself in a dark alley."

Cara's cheeks went pink. "I'm standing right here."

"Did I seem confused about that? I wasn't." Meredith crossed her arms and glared at Keith. "Watch yourself. I see that look in your eye. I'm the one who held her while she cried over your worthless hide. Don't you dare break her heart again or the sharks out there will be mysteriously well fed."

"Still here." Cara smacked Meredith but she didn't budge.

They were the same height in their sky-high heels, with the same nose and long, sooty eyelashes, but the similarity ended there. Meredith was a traffic-stopper with her obvious, in-your-face assets, where Cara had a refined beauty that had snared Keith's attention the moment he'd locked gazes with her across the bar, back in Houston. He hadn't even noticed Meredith sitting on the next stool when he'd beelined it over to introduce himself and buy Cara a drink.

Keith saluted Meredith. "Yes, ma'am. No dark alleys. No broken hearts."

"I'm serious, Mitchell." She stuck V-ed fingers near her eyeballs and flipped them around to stab at Keith. "I'm watching you."

"Don't worry your pretty little head about Cara. I'm here to do a job and that's my sole focus."

"Uh-huh. And I'm just here for the pool boys."

With that, she flounced off, leaving him alone with Cara. She wore the same thing she'd had on earlier, which he'd had difficulty fully appreciating in a dark elevator. The lightweight summer skirt and tailored blouse accentuated her curves just as well as the jogging outfit from their pre-dawn run and the outfit's deep shade of peach naturally led to a desire to take a bite out of the creamy swell of her cleavage.

The outside temperature heated, though he'd have sworn it was a balmy eighty degrees five seconds ago. Learning she wasn't a liar and manipulator stirred things below the belt in different, unanticipated ways. Coupled with a brand-new entrepreneur's skin, Cara was suddenly a full package he wanted to rip open with enthusiasm.

She rolled her eyes with amusement. "Meredith has Mama's flair for melodrama. Among other things."

"I've always liked your sister. You like her, too."

"I couldn't do this design business without her." She glanced at him with a slow sweep that dialed up his awareness of how very much he liked dressed-to-the-nines Cara. "Did you want something?"

Yes, he did. It just wasn't the same thing he'd wanted when he left the meeting. "How is your ankle?"

"That's what you chased me down to ask?"

The breeze picked up and flung strands of hair into her face, which he did not hesitate to smooth back. She froze under his fingers. What was he doing? "I'm concerned about you. You're an integral part of the expo."

"I'm fine. I doubt I'll be jogging in the morning. But I'm okay."

"Now that's a crying shame." He'd been looking forward to running side by side with natural Cara, oddly enough. Jogging was supposed to be a solitary sport. That's why he liked it.

His phone vibrated and as he was still on the job, he pulled it out. And swore.

"Problem?" she asked.

"Potentially. I've had my eye on a depression in the Atlantic for a week or so. NOAA just upgraded it to Tropical Storm Mark." He flashed his phone toward her, showing her the map sent by the National Oceanic and Atmospheric Administration. "NOAA app."

"Who has an NOAA app?"

"A consultant hired to turn around a resort located on the leading edge of the Caribbean during hurricane season. I'm good at what I do."

Cara's gaze skittered across his mouth, lingering. "I'm pretty aware of the breadth of your skill set."

Her voice had dropped, turning sultry, and his body hardened in an instant. Yeah, he remembered how hot their kisses had always been. If he could find a way to make up for his mistake, maybe she'd be interested in a repeat of the fun, expectation-free part of their past.

"Are you flirting with me, Cara?"

She smiled and Meredith's shark threat seemed less treacherous in comparison. "Not in the slightest. Your best skill is walking away and I took copious notes. Allow me to demonstrate what I learned."

She pivoted on one sexy stiletto and hobbled after Meredith, leaving Keith standing alone by the pool.

With a tropical storm on the horizon and a grand reopening combined with a bridal expo in two days, Cara was a distraction he could ill afford to indulge. Their history was painful and irreconcilable. Probably too difficult to overcome, regardless of whether she'd actually forgiven him.

Nonetheless, her pointed refusal to engage fanned the flames of his competitive streak into a full-fledged blaze. Once, he'd been eager to disentangle himself from a wannabe trophy wife with zero ambition, and now he could think of nothing else but exploring the new, uncharted Cara.

Keith Mitchell did not back down from a challenge.

Three

"What do you mean the flight was canceled?" Cara dropped to the bed and flung both shoes at the wall. Since she was a lover not a pitcher, her Louboutins clunked to the carpet well short of the intended target. Just as everything else she'd attempted to do since landing on this island impersonating paradise.

Meredith pushed a couple of buttons on the coffee brewer—her second pot of the day. "C-A-N-C—"

"I know how to spell canceled, smart aleck. *Why* is the flight canceled?"

Her sister shrugged. "Mechanical failure. Pilot's strike. Lost in the Bermuda Triangle. Take your pick. Does it matter? You can wear the dress in the show and I'll run things backstage. People will love the designer taking the runway. Stop freaking out."

"I have to freak out. It's what I do." Cara had already sent Jackie home and the replacement model should have landed at Providenciales Airport an hour ago. Except her flight out of JFK was canceled.

"Let Keith bring you that bottle of wine he offered. You need to relax."

"One day, I'll learn to stop repeating my conversations to you verbatim." Cara scowled and rubbed her ankle, which was not fine despite all her insistence to *that man*. Mentally, she scrolled through her shoe inventory and gave up. Except for her jogging shoes, she'd brought nothing less than three-and-a-half-inch heels. She might not even *own* anything less than three. "I have no interest in being anywhere near Keith."

"I'll drink it then. The bottle he sent last night was not bad."

Cara wouldn't know. She'd refused to let one drop grace her lips. "You can fantasize about him, too, if you want. Or sleep with him. I don't care."

Meredith jerked to a halt, halfway across the room. "Oh, honey. I had no idea you still had feelings for him. Don't clue him in just yet, okay? Make him work for it."

"I don't still have feelings for him!" Cara fell face-first into the raw-silk comforter. Such a vehement denial probably didn't help her case any. Rolling, she stared at the ceiling.

Mad, she had plenty of. Summoning it up took no effort at all.

She frowned when it didn't happen. Well, hell. She might not be as pissed as she used to be, not anymore. He'd been so weird in the elevator after she'd laid into him about being such a sleaze. Weird and speechless, and Keith didn't usually do speechless. He always had words at the tip of his tongue.

That's how she knew he'd told the truth about why he left. And she should have told him about the miscarriage right then and there in her dressing room, regardless of how upset and disoriented she'd been. They'd both made mistakes—his obviously being a lot more flagrant and inexcusable—but it was over with and she had a job to do.

Cara sat up. "I have alterations and so do you. Thanks for being a pit bull earlier and I really appreciated the shark warning, but nothing is going to happen with Keith. In fact, the name *Keith Mitchell* is henceforth banned from being said. Keith Mitchell is like Voldemort to you."

"Creepy on the outside but looks like Ralph Fiennes underneath and has a delish accent?" Meredith waggled her brows.

"Shut up. I'm doing my alterations on the beach. The waves are relaxing, aren't they?" Cara gathered her sewing kit and folded the dress into a bag while Meredith snickered through dumping half a sugar refinery into her coffee.

"Then I'm doing my alterations at the pool. Maybe Paolo will be back, now that your boyfriend's not there to scare him off. Don't wait up," Meredith called after Cara as she exited their hotel room.

The beach was deserted. Everyone currently staying at the resort had a behind-the-scenes role in the bridal expo. The real guests were the wedding professionals who would arrive for the grand opening at the end of the week and then attend the expo featuring the latest wedding trends.

Cara had her pick of beach loungers and arranged a plastic tarp over several to lay out the dress, careful to keep it away from the sand, though the entire expo would take place on the beach. Sand was inevitable. The alterations weren't extensive but she'd handmade all her dresses and every stitch had to be redone carefully. No sewing machine quick fixes for Cara Chandler-Harris Designs.

If the bridal expo worked to increase business as she planned, sewing machines would be a necessary part of her future. Standing orders meant she couldn't take a month to make one dress any longer. Cara threaded a needle and reminded herself she welcomed the influx of business and the opportunity, though Meredith had to convince her of it daily.

This was Cara's life now. She stabbed the needle through the silk spread out over her lap. Weddings were for other women, not her, regardless of how much she wished otherwise. Cara couldn't imagine trusting a man enough to fall in love, let alone marry him. Every day, she expected to wake up and realize she'd gotten over her caution.

Hadn't happened yet. Until then, she'd sew. The surf crashed a few feet away and the cry of gulls floated on a light afternoon breeze. Her life did not suck. She'd found a way to be content instead of deliriously happy, and it was enough.

Sometime later, a shadow fell over the tiny new stitches. Cara glanced up and cursed her stupid quivery heart for lurching even a little bit over the sight of Keith. But sweet Jesus did that man fill out a suit, and he had charm and wit to spare. Once upon a time, she'd thoroughly enjoyed his company.

"Busy?" he asked.

"Nah. I'm working on my tan."

"Sorry, that was a stupid question." He sat without invitation on the next lounger, their knees nearly touching, and his eyes trained on her bare feet. "Is your ankle still bothering you?"

"Geez. That was a lame excuse to talk to me the first twelve times. What's really going on in that pretty little head of yours?"

He grinned and her polarized sunglasses did nothing to protect her from the dazzle. "Do I need an excuse to talk to you?"

"No, you need to take a number. Can't you see how popular I am?" She waved at the empty beach. "Sandals and sand don't mix, ironically enough. That's why I'm barefoot. Stop asking me about my ankle."

Weakness in any form bothered her, especially around Keith, who could scent weakness with the precision of a homing device. Meredith's shark scenario was sweet, but ineffective. Sharks never ate their own kind.

She sighed. Keith wasn't quite the heartless bastard she'd been telling herself for two years. She'd have to stop thinking of him as one.

"Then I'll go with a different excuse. Have dinner with me."

She couldn't help it. Laughter bubbled out before she could choke it back. "No, really. What do you want?"

"That is what I want. But in lieu of that, I'll settle for your advice. The resort wedding coordinator quit with no notice. Her first task was to organize a mock wedding for the expo, and it's in shambles. Is there any way you could walk through the plans with one of the management staff?"

She stared at Keith's inscrutable expression. "You want my help?"

"Desperately and I'm not afraid to beg. I'd compensate you for your time."

Her soul thrilled a little at the thought of a big bucket of masculinity like Keith on his knees, begging. She was five-eight, but even in heels, she never got to be taller than him.

"Money's not the object of my hesitation. It's more that you're asking me for a favor." That brought her up short. He'd owe her. Big-time. And she'd already started thinking of ways to collect, starting with a brand-new fantasy involving Keith and his knees. "Why would you ask me, out of all the people here?"

"Because you've planned a wedding."

"That's rich, Mitchell. How convenient."

"It's not a matter of convenience. I've seen what you can do, and no one else could possibly hope to meet my standards. Except you." Those caramel eyes were on hers, all melty and scrumptious and saying far more than his mouth did.

"So now my ability to plan a wedding is a hot commodity. As I recall, you weren't so keen on it before." She waited for the sting of anger, but it had really and truly fled, dang it. When she'd told him she'd forgiven him in the elevator, it had mostly been because she couldn't resist being contrary, but it seemed to have stuck.

And he wanted her help with *wedding planning*. Nothing got her more excited. Well, almost nothing.

"I can't redo the past. But I can make it up to you now. Name it. Your wish is my command." His scalding gaze rested on her feet again and her toes tingled. She dug them down into the sand where he couldn't see them.

"Don't worry about it." She had absolutely zero desire to find out how he intended to make it up to her. Okay, maybe ten percent desire, but strictly out of curiosity. "I'll help you, but I'll be very demanding and difficult to work with."

His knee swung closer to hers, grazing it as he leaned forward. "Which is no less than I expect. Thanks."

Her breath caught. Of all things, Keith's knee was turning her insides flippy, way down low where all the really neglected parts had throbbed to life. "When do you need me?"

"Right now." That caramel gaze boiled over with searing intensity, holding her captive.

Heat blazed, nearly singeing her uncovered skin. The covered places were pretty hot too and straining to be free of their confines. "You can have me for an hour. Is that long enough?"

"I can accomplish plenty with you in an hour."

Her tongue came out to wet parched lips, and every nerve was screaming to feel his mouth against them instead. "We're still talking about the same thing, right?"

He held out a hand and God above, she was afraid to take it. But she did. He drew her forward, oh so slowly, into his space, where it smelled like ocean and Keith. "I sincerely hope so."

"Great," she croaked and jerked back out of the danger zone. "Let me put my dress in the room and grab my shoes. I'll meet your staff member at the front desk."

"I'll tell her to expect you." He let her pull away, never breaking eye contact as their flesh separated. "And Cara? You and I both know that's not what we were talking about."

She fled before her neglected parts overruled her brain.

By the time she reached her room, she was breathless and mad at herself.

So Keith was hot and really, really, really good at making her body hum. Everything down there needed to *shut up*. This wasn't a vacation and they both had a lot of work to do. Plus, he scared the crap out of her. She'd been down that path and it was not lined with primrose.

The man had serious commitment issues. Her heart wasn't up for another beating, and she could never have a casual tropical island fling with Keith Mitchell. Not then, not now. They were total opposites in that regard. He wasn't interested in long-term. She was.

Besides, Keith had superhero sperm, capable of leaping tall birth control methods. She wasn't even on the pill this time. Abstinence was the only method guaranteed to work.

The reasons for steering clear were piled so high, she couldn't see over them even if she put on a pair of ten-inch heels.

Meredith was gone, thank goodness. Cara so did not want to have another conversation about he-who-must-not-be-named, and on top of that, her sister could read her like an instruction manual. Cara was genuinely afraid of what must be written all over her face—her runaway groom admitted he needed her and praised her wedding-planning efforts at the same time.

That flipped her insides much more powerfully than any heated gaze Keith could shoot in her direction.

Keith waited for Cara at the front desk and shot off some emails so he didn't look like a lovesick teenager hanging out in hopes of accidentally running into the object of his affection. Of course, the things he wanted to do to Cara had a decidedly adult theme. All that heat on the beach had definitely not been one-sided, but she apparently planned to pretend otherwise.

He didn't. This expo would get 100 percent of his attention during working hours, but there was nothing wrong with some after-hours relaxation with an old flame, was there?

Clacking heels announced Cara's arrival, but his Y chromosome had scented her the moment she stepped through the lobby doors. That peach outfit hadn't grown any less mouthwatering as the day wore on, and the sea breeze had teased her hair into a tumbled mess his fingers strained to dive into.

The rest of the lobby vanished. All he could see was Cara.

"I'm here," she said.

Yes, she was. There must be something in the salt air because the first time they'd been together, being in her presence did not drive him batty. Chemistry, they had, but he'd always been able to focus when she wasn't around. Now? Not so much.

And when she was around…well, he was allowing her to be so much of a distraction, he should hand in his resignation to Regent before the sun set.

Or he could get his mind out of Cara's cleavage and act

like the professional he'd insisted she be. Thus far, he'd been the one who'd devolved.

The resort's assistant manager, a native islander who'd been working in local resorts for fifteen years, came around from behind the front desk for an introduction. "Mary Kwane, this is Cara," Keith said. "Mary is filling in until we can hire another wedding coordinator."

Mary sized up Cara and offered her hand. "What are your qualifications?"

Cara shook the other woman's hand and smiled. "I planned a wedding in two months."

"How many guests?" Mary didn't mince words but her work ethic was unparalleled. He hired only the best.

"Five hundred, with two venues and two different themes."

Keith did a double take. Really? Conceptualizing two separate themes was ridiculous, but he eyed Cara with new respect, nonetheless, because she'd also done it while pregnant. Without his help.

Then, because of him, she hadn't gotten to enjoy any of it. His stomach rolled. He'd given lip service to making it up to her, but that wasn't actually possible. Yet she'd let it go, as if he'd done nothing more serious than misplace her favorite earrings.

"I'll leave the two of you to it," he said and escaped.

Keith met with Elena so he and the resort manager could formulate a plan to fill the vacant wedding coordinator position and then he spent an hour alone in his office buried in procurement paperwork. In the next room, Alice and a couple of additional team members slashed through the pages-long to-do list, communicating their progress via chat windows. Keith glanced through the updates periodically while he pretended not to be dwelling on Cara.

Probably he should forget about how gorgeous and tantalizing and challenging she was. He'd done nothing to reconcile his screwup, and her *back-off* sign couldn't be any larger.

A reminder beeped on his phone but he didn't need it. Today was his mom's birthday and with the time difference between here and Miami, he should catch her before she started preparing for an evening on the town. His father escorted her to the opera and dinner every year like clockwork.

She picked up on the forth ring.

"Hi, Mom. Happy birthday."

"Keith. How nice of you to call," she said coolly as if he never called, which was patently false. "Are you enjoying Turks and Caicos? I prefer Bali this time of year but Grace Bay is satisfactory for a weekend getaway, I suppose."

Cara is here, Mom. At the resort. Yes, she's still a knock-out but different, too. Unexpectedly so. I have no idea what to do about her.

"I'm working," Keith said. "I'm not on vacation."

Mitchells didn't *work*; they made money as passively as possible. Neither of his parents understood his drive to break family tradition and actually get his hands dirty. The most immersing activity his dad had done in the past twenty years was browse through the prospectus of the multibillion-dollar portfolio he'd amassed as a hedge fund manager. Following in his father's footsteps was about as attractive to Keith as sucking up Florida swamp water with a straw.

A strong work ethic, the satisfaction of tangible results and the pride of making his own way—these were the things that got Keith out of bed in the morning. Not money. Money was strictly a reward for following his own path. His father had never understood that and expressed his disappointment in Keith's lack of interest in Wall Street on a routine basis.

"How's the weather?" he asked.

"Dreadful. I was just telling your father that the humidity is suffocating me."

"Did you get the gift I sent?" Alice had sent it but it was the same thing.

"Of course. It was lovely. I'd have preferred you bring it in person, but you're too busy *working.*"

Keith stifled a sigh. If he recorded this conversation, he could play it back and skip the actual phone call next time. "I'll visit soon. Maybe next month after the resort opens."

Visits were to be endured. Much like the calls, but he did both with frequency because it meant something to his parents. What, he couldn't fathom. They were essentially polite strangers who shared a last name. They never discussed personal feelings or anything of substance. Such was their relationship and always had been.

"Your father is having chest pains again." His father always had chest pains because he refused to stop eating spicy food, but his mom had never met a guilt trip she didn't like to bestow on her only child. "Don't dally, or it might be too late this time."

Cara's running her own business, which I know doesn't impress you since you've never acknowledged how hard I've worked to do the same. If it didn't sound so patronizing, I'd tell her I'm proud of her.

He longed to say the words aloud, longed to talk to someone who really cared about his thoughts and dreams and disappointments.

"There's a tropical storm developing," he advised, well against his better judgment, but he'd sleep better for it. "Keep an eye on the Weather Channel. Tropical Storm Mark. It's headed northwest toward the Bahamas and could hit Miami after that as a category one."

"Oh, they couldn't forecast where a shoe was going to drop if they held it out in front of them."

"Have a nice time at the opera, Mom. Give my regards to Dad."

Keith disconnected the call and put his parents out of his mind. The loneliness the call had sparked wasn't so easily dismissed. But that was the price of his lifestyle.

Ten minutes later, Elisabeth sent him a text message about a problem with spa services, which immediately sparked an idea he would have thought of earlier if he'd been on his game. It wasn't nearly enough to balance his mental ledger, but it was a start.

Shoving away from his desk, he went in search of Cara and Mary. They were having a heated conversation at a conference table in one of the resort meeting rooms.

"Brides don't want someone picking out their flowers for them," Cara said, so sweetly he'd have thought she and Mary were lifelong friends. Except you'd need a chain saw to cut the tension in the room.

"They do if they come to Grace Bay. It's a destination wedding, not a church wedding. The couples will not be able to select everything ahead of time." Mary drummed her long nails on the table but the lilt in her island accent had elongated, giving away her irritation before she'd finished speaking.

"Honey, that's what the internet is for. Put up pictures."

"We don't have the budget for an interactive web—"

Mary glanced up when Keith cleared his throat. "I thought you were discussing the mock expo wedding. Not the resort's wedding services."

"You can't separate one from the other," Cara said with a syrupy smile at Mary. "You invited editors of bridal magazines to the expo. They're going to do a write-up of the mock wedding. Next month, an engaged woman sees the spread, thinks 'Yes, that's *exactly* what I want,' only to find out the mock wedding doesn't resemble the real thing the resort offers. How would you feel about explaining this discrepancy to Regent executives?"

Keith closed his mouth before it started gathering flies. "Excellent point."

Arms crossed, Mary shot both him and Cara a glare. "Maybe you should start working on your explanation for Regent executives about the expense of her grandiose notions."

He had a better idea. "Mary, I'd like a report detailing the resort's proposed wedding services. Work with Alice to pull the budget numbers and post the report to the document collaboration site in one hour. Cara, come with me."

Wariness crept across Cara's expression. "I'm not finished here."

"You are for now. I'll review Mary's report and we'll reconvene in the morning. Thank you both for your spirited commitment." He bit his tongue to keep from smiling at their scowls. Women and weddings. Mix the two and stand back.

Mary left to find Alice, and a quick text message to his admin explained the emergency interruption he'd just sent her way. Cara leaned back in the conference room chair and crossed her bare legs in defiance instead of standing so they could go.

"Is your macho card worn out yet?" she asked.

He didn't bother to stop the grin now that they were alone. "Not quite. I have a few days left before it expires. Come on. Or do you need me to carry you?"

She crossed her arms, which did not help his mind stay out of her cleavage since it was so nicely framed and jutting upward. "Where are we going?"

"It's a surprise."

Her mulish expression didn't change. "I'm not having dinner with you. I have a lot of work to do and apparently will be spending more of my precious time tomorrow doing your job. Unless the surprise involves wine and a bubble bath, keep it."

"It does." Smoothly, he bent down and extracted her from the chair, pulling her to her feet. "The manager of spa services needs a guinea pig with high-end tastes to evaluate the recently added staff. I immediately thought of you."

"That was a backhanded compliment if I ever heard one," she groused, but her face lit up and the sledgehammer took aim at his gut. She was inches away, close enough to get a hint of her perfume, which wound through his brain like an opiate.

One small movement forward by either of them would draw their bodies together. And his hadn't gotten the message to forget about how much he wanted to take a slow, leisurely tour of her cleavage.

"I think she mentioned champagne." He cleared the catch from his raw, burning throat. He should step back. Into the next room. The next building, before he started breaking her back-off sign into tiny little pieces.

"Lead the way."

Golden flecks in her espresso irises had him pinned. He couldn't look away. "You're not too busy?"

"For the spa? Never." Her husky voice whispered from parted lips and he was acutely aware that if there was any breaking going on, it was to his sanity.

He rocked on the ball of his foot and at the last instant moved back. Not forward. "It's this way."

His senses buzzed as they crossed the pool deck to the spa building overlooking the beach. The late-afternoon sun cast everything in shadow. It was going to be a long, long, frustrating night, he suspected.

Keith introduced Cara to the spa manager, Elisabeth, a diminutive French transplant from another Regent property in the Canaries, and turned to leave.

"Where are you going?" Cara asked.

"Back to work." As always.

Elisabeth excused herself to prepare the technicians as Cara spread a graceful hand across his chest and shoved. He took a step back to humor her.

"Not so fast, Mitchell. We have much to discuss. Besides, your tastes are just as high-end as mine."

"Are you suggesting I be a guinea pig, as well? A spa day is not on my to-do list." Neither was listening to her ream him again for his crimes. His subconscious was doing a fine job of that without additional input.

"Mine either. But here I am, doing you yet another favor. The least you can do is listen to what I have to say about the wedding services. Mary is going to make all kinds of mistakes."

That was a different kettle of fish. If she wanted to discuss her ideas, that counted as work. "Fine. I'll stay. But I'm not getting a manicure. I'll be the unobtrusive one in the corner."

"Ha. You're as unobtrusive as an elephant in a lingerie store."

Elisabeth, who had returned, broke in. "They're ready for you."

She guided Keith to a plush suede chair and settled Cara into a matching one across the aisle. Three smocked women with various instruments of torture in their hands swarmed around it, chattering to each other, to Cara, to Elisabeth, doing things to Cara's nails and face and completely ignoring him. He was content to watch, especially when one of the ladies drew off Cara's shoes and plunked her feet in a tub of soapy water.

After a few minutes of soaking, the technician began working her thumbs into the arch of Cara's bare foot and Keith was mildly ashamed of how erotic his lower half seemed to find the whole scene.

"Elisabeth." He jerked his head, indicating she should

come closer. In a low voice, he said, "Tell your girl to be careful with Cara's left ankle. She twisted it earlier today."

"Yes, sir." Elisabeth repeated the instructions to the technician, which Cara clearly overheard. She narrowed her eyes at Keith and stuck her tongue out.

"I thought you wanted to talk," he called to her.

"That was before I knew your magicians were going to melt my bones." Her eyelids drifted closed and pure bliss radiated from her body. "But I know you're busy, so listen up."

His own body bristled in response, and little licks of lust tormented him for the next thirty minutes while Cara outlined all the problems she'd identified with the previous wedding coordinator's plans, which he and Elena had approved long ago. Then she launched into an impassioned explanation of ideas involving flowers, honeymoon packages and the *pièce de résistance*—butterflies. Despite being overly fanciful, Cara was on the mark.

He would have to take all of this into consideration, along with Mary's report. Tomorrow.

The technicians finally put away their instruments and helped Cara from the chair. As she stood, she wobbled on unsteady legs. Any reasonable man would put an arm around her to keep her off the tile, and Keith prided himself on being reasonable.

She snugged up next to his torso, comfortably, which shouldn't come as a shock—their bodies knew each other. Intimately. Two years hadn't been nearly long enough to forget the curve of her waist and how beautifully it nipped in at the juncture below his palm.

Once they cleared the door of the spa, he realized how late it had gotten. The sky was in the throes of a spectacular sunset, bleeding orange, pink and yellow into the horizon in all directions. The water had darkened to deep blue and a cool breeze wafted inland across the sand.

"Nice timing, Mitchell. A girl might think you planned it this way."

A laugh scraped his dry throat. "As much as I appreciate the compliment, even I can't control nature."

She stepped out of his embrace and his side cooled much too quickly. "The spa was nice. Thanks."

"I'd like to do more."

"I just bet you would." She swept him once with an amused glance. "Is this when you were going to casually mention the late hour and suggest we grab a quick bite to eat?"

It was now. "You have to eat sometime."

"Not with you I don't." She whirled and started hobbling off but he caught her easily, backing her up against the side of the building, scant inches separating his chest from her rapidly rising and falling breasts.

She met his gaze boldly as he braced both hands against the stucco on each side of her neck. "Going somewhere, Cara?"

His body, still galvanized from watching her enjoy ministrations at the hands of another, snarled for release to plunge in.

"I have a date." She licked her lips and he nearly came apart. "And it's not with you."

A growl rumbled in his chest. "Cancel it."

"I don't want to."

Stay. I want to spend time with you. Get to know the real *you, the person you've become.*

He leaned in a centimeter and her breasts quivered as she sucked in a breath. "Sure about that? You know it's only a matter of time before I have my hands on you. Here." He traced a line down her throat and stopped short of the luscious, mounded V of her cleavage. He'd keep going in a heartbeat if she gave the slightest sign she'd welcome it.

The past, his mistakes, the emotional responses she kept

pulling from him—all of that was too complicated. But this heat between them he knew precisely how to deal with.

He pressed closer.

"Take a cold shower," she advised with raised brows. "Feels like you could use one."

His erection had obviously caught her notice. It would have been hard to miss. "Take one with me."

I don't want to be alone right now.

"Doesn't that sort of defeat the purpose?" She blinked, breaking their locked gazes. "Let's cut to the chase. I'm not interested. I can't begin to understand why you'd think otherwise."

With the slightest tilt of his hips, he nudged the soft flesh of her abdomen, and those amazing rosy lips parted in a raspy exhale that he felt all the way down to his knees.

"I'm reading between the lines."

"Keith," she breathed and lifted her chin, bringing her face to within a millimeter of his. His lungs forgot to function and he flattened both palms against the stucco to hold himself upright. "You know what's between the lines? Space. Same as what's between your hands."

She ducked under his braced arm with ease and walked away. Without limping.

Four

That night, Cara slept poorly. She'd have liked to blame it on Meredith's vampire-like schedule, but when the sun finally rose, she didn't have the heart to gripe about her sister's late-night rendezvous or her 3:00 a.m. return to their room that had sounded like a gazelle learning to ride a bike.

It wasn't Meredith's fault Cara was restless. That award went to the master of reading between the lines, dang it. Why did Keith have to be so delicious and so hard to walk away from?

She rolled from bed and wished she'd indulged in at least one glass of wine the night before to go with the hangover quality of this morning. Two cups of coffee and a shower did not improve her mood.

"Time to get up." Cara yanked the covers off the still-sleeping lump in her sister's bed.

Meredith stretched like a sated cat and blinked. "Mmm. Good morning to you, too. Any coffee left?"

"You're entirely too perky for someone who's had five hours of sleep."

"You'd be perky too after the night I had." Meredith waggled her brows. "Paolo worked at a resort in Phuket and let me tell you, Thailand must be the place to learn a few tricks, if you get my drift."

"Your drift is as subtle as a nuclear bomb," Cara said drily. "We have a lot of work to do today, and somehow I got roped into helping he-who-must-not-be-named with the mock wedding."

"Yeah. Somehow." Meredith grinned and flounced to the shower, buck naked and not at all ashamed. Of course, when you looked like a centerfold, what was there to hide?

Cara sighed and got to work on the alterations she hadn't finished yesterday thanks to the side trip to the spa. Which had been very nice indeed and had totally worked the kinks out of her ankle. She had a feeling Keith had meant the spa session as some kind of treat, despite his insistence the "services" needed testing.

So maybe both were true. It didn't matter. She needed to stop thinking about Keith and especially stop remembering the good parts of their relationship. There was no scenario in which that would end well.

She stuck the needle through the dress's fabric and focused on how this creation would transform one of her models into a beautiful bride. Eventually, a real bride might want this same dress and Cara would gladly restitch it to fit its future owner. These dresses *weren't* one-use-only, no matter what Keith tried to claim, and regardless, Cara filled a bride's critical need by helping her have the most memorable day possible.

Cara Chandler-Harris Designs filled a need, too—it gave her the sense of belonging she craved. One day, marriage would give her that. Until then, she'd sew.

When Keith texted her an hour later, the sight of his

name on her phone's screen put a sharp thrill in her midsection. Quickly, she squelched it. What was wrong with her?

"I'm going to meet Keith at the beach," Cara called to Meredith casually. "You can stay here and keep working on the dresses."

"Are you out of your mind?" Meredith stood so fast, a box of thread crashed to the floor. "I'm not missing this."

Cara strangled over a groan. "It's not a show. We're just going over the basic plan for the mock wedding. The expo starts tomorrow, and these dresses are not going to alter themselves."

"Honey, whenever you and Keith are in the same room, it's always a show." Her sister carefully folded the dress in front of her. "And I never said I wasn't going to do alterations while I was watching."

Cara let it go, mostly because she wasn't sure why she'd protested in the first place. It wasn't as if she'd wanted to be alone with Keith. The opposite was a much saner idea anyway. The buffer of Meredith would be a blessing in disguise.

When the two women reached the beach, it was teeming with people. Had she missed a memo? She could have sworn Keith had said he was short staffed and needed her help.

The wind picked up and blew Cara's hair into her mouth as she zeroed in on the tallest man present. And she'd deny to her grave that she'd noticed him the moment she'd hit the edge of the beach.

"What's all this?" she asked.

"We need to run through the ceremony." Keith waved at the crowd without glancing in Cara's direction and barked out an order to a passing member of the catering staff. "These are all the participants."

All righty then. She squared her shoulders.

"Let's get to work. You." Cara put a hand on the shoulder

of a baby-faced guy walking by. "We need white wooden chairs set up in two parallel sections on each side of the walkway leading to the gazebo. Find them. Set them up in about ten rows. Come tell me when you're done."

That got Keith's attention. His gaze swung around to zero in on her as the errand boy snapped off a "Yes, ma'am."

Keith grinned and it swirled up a hot jumble in her midsection.

"That was the sexiest thing I've ever heard uttered in a large crowd," he drawled and crossed his arms. "Do it again."

Coolly, she smiled back so he didn't guess that his appreciation affected her far more greatly than it should have. "You. Go find Mary and ask her for the preselected flowers she's so fond of. Be nice or she'll pinch the heads off just to spite me. She can get them to the beach herself or assign someone, I don't care. I just need them pronto."

"Here's where you get to be impressed with how efficient I am." With a wink, Keith sent a quick text message and pocketed his phone. "Next?"

Cara's smile grew into something a little more genuine, even though she'd devised the task with the strict intent of making Keith disappear for a minute or two while she got herself under control. "Are you actually letting me tell you what to do?"

"Until it stops being sexy." He shrugged good-naturedly. "I expect that'll take a while. Plus, I asked you to help. I have no problem if that translates into you being in charge. Feel free to order me around at will."

Keith raked her with a once-over that easily conveyed his willingness to continue that philosophy in whatever venue she chose. Heat flushed her skin and sparked at her core, where nothing should be sparking.

"Music," she murmured, calling on all her debutante blood to get the word out. If she'd learned anything from

Mama, it was how to put on a crowd face when you were anything but settled inside. "Recorded or live?"

"Recorded for now." His gaze was riveted to her lips and she felt a rush as if he'd actually bent his head, aiming his mouth toward hers.

That was the cause of her sleepless night. She'd dreamed of Keith closing that gap and kissing her as he used to, with masterful skill and mind-altering power.

Neither of them had moved but the sand beneath her feet seemed to shift, falling away at an alarming rate. It was useless to pretend she wasn't interested when both of them knew it was a lie.

"Mr. Mitchell."

They jolted and turned in unison to the speaker. One of the many groundskeepers launched into a question. Keith rattled off the answer and then turned to survey the beach, where a mock wedding was now spontaneously forming around them. But not before she caught a flash of guilt on his face.

God above, what was she doing letting such a moment draw out here in front of everyone? They both had a job to do. As if the job was the biggest issue to why that charged, simmering moment was a not-good-very-bad idea.

"You," she muttered under her breath to herself. "Get your mind out of Keith's boxer briefs and focus."

Keith must have given himself the same stern lecture because he didn't meet her eyes for the next two hours as they worked seamlessly side by side to put wedding props in place around the stationary gazebo anchored to the sand by four concrete pylons. Slowly the area took shape, but the wind kept carrying away the rose petals Mary had strewn down the aisle between the white chairs.

"Why in the world did you plan this expo in September?" Cara groused to Keith after one of the torchères lining the aisle blew over. Fortunately, it wasn't lit yet. Otherwise they'd be facing an out-of-control fire.

"September is the slowest time of year. Because of the weather," Keith said without batting an eye. "And I need the resort opened by October. So we'll deal with our friend Tropical Storm Mark and pray it veers away."

As he'd claimed very clearly last night, even Mitchell the Missile couldn't control nature.

The concern in his voice was so evident, it gave her a strange desire to make things easier for him in whatever capacity she could. "There's enough set up to run through a ceremony. Who volunteered to be the bride and groom?"

A wolfish gleam in his eyes set her spine tingling. He held out his hand. "We did. Will you do me the honor of being my stand-in bride?"

Cara fought the urge to laugh hysterically. "Might as well keep up the trend."

Always the bride, but never married. Story of her life.

When Cara took Keith's hand as if she actually intended to play Holy Matrimony with him, he barely caught the shock before it spilled into his expression.

He'd expected her to stick her nose in the air and tell him to find another bride. Because he'd been kidding.

"Are you giving the deal a thumbs-up?" he asked.

She should say no, especially considering the point of this exercise was to practice for the mock wedding scheduled for the expo later in the week. It would be hard to evaluate the process while in the middle of it.

Actually, she should say no simply because he'd already burned her once in the wedding department. And because the sensual heat sizzling the atmosphere was starting to make him sweat.

"Sure, why not?" Cara jerked her head toward the metal gazebo wrapped with blooms that had taken her and Mary forty-five minutes to arrange. "It's about time I see what all the fuss is about."

It was a not-so-subtle reminder that she hadn't gotten to participate in her own wedding, and remorse over his role in the fiasco took on a new low. But if she was making a joke, she must really be over it.

He risked a joke of his own. "Looks like you're going to get me down the aisle after all."

She smirked. "Looks like I got you to help plan the ceremony after all."

Touché. They exchanged grins, and the weight Keith had been carrying since the elevator lessened all at once. Why wedding jokes had accomplished that above anything else, he couldn't say. What had he done to deserve both her help and absolution?

They were still holding hands, not that Keith would point it out and lose the tenuous connection with a woman he definitely didn't know as well as he wanted to.

"Shall we get all our guests in order?" Keith suggested.

"You take the guests. I'll handle the music and the officiant." She let her hands slide from his and his palm grew cool.

He watched Cara corral Meredith and the pool boy attached to her sister's hip into handling the portable music system. Cara's face glowed with purpose, and the silk sleeveless blouse she wore V-ed over her chest so nicely, it was hard to tear his gaze away. With regret, he turned to handle his appointed task, also sorry he hadn't suggested testing out the honeymoon suite afterward.

But that was for the best. Probably. She'd just shut him down again and his ego was still a little bruised from last night.

In a matter of minutes, fifty or so of his employees had taken their seats and the stand-in officiant stood under the gazebo. After opening day, Regent would utilize a handful of freelance wedding officials who worked with the local resorts on a couple-by-couple basis, but for now, Cara had solicited the help of what appeared to be one of the chefs.

Cara waited for Keith at the head of the aisle, clutching a spray of flowers Mary thrust into her hands. Meredith hit Play on the recorded music and something string-laden and weepy filled the air. The wind died down a bit in apparent reverence for the occasion—and checking this particular task off his ever-growing list definitely constituted an occasion in Keith's book.

He walked down the aisle and ignored all the grinning faces aimed in his direction. No doubt they loved the opportunity to see their boss in a starring role. The price of an ill-timed and ill-conceived joke.

Cara's smile, on the other hand, hit him hard. Framed by the flowered gazebo and breathtaking ocean, she had never been more stunning. Out of nowhere, the image of her in her wedding dress popped into his head and superimposed itself over the woman several yards away.

She'd been beautiful then, too—as were the decorations she'd selected—but he vastly preferred this wedding, and not just because he'd still be single at the end of it. Maybe it was the beach, or the minimal props, but the ceremony had a much more free-form feel to it, lighter and with less expectation. Exactly as he'd envisioned for both the mock expo wedding and the long-term resort wedding services.

Cara had done an exceptional job. Not that he was surprised. Keith was good at what he did and he'd have never asked her to organize the wedding if he'd thought Cara would fail.

Okay, maybe he was a little surprised. But only over the fact that Cara had nailed this task he'd dropped on her, which hit all the right notes. In-charge Cara rocked his socks.

He joined Cara at the end of the aisle with a mental list

of small adjustments—the sand needed to be raked prior to the ceremony, the chef couldn't be the officiant in the mock wedding because he'd be otherwise occupied and Cara should definitely stop smiling at him like that.

It was messing with his ability to concentrate.

"What's got you so thrilled?" he asked brusquely. "This is all fake, you know."

"Ah, but you're wrong." She speared him with a heated glance that he couldn't have misinterpreted even if someone had blindfolded him. "I can see it on your face. This is exactly what you wanted out of the mock wedding. Which means you owe me one. And when I collect, it's going to feel very real to you indeed."

That had all sorts of interesting possibilities threaded through it and sounded distinctly opposite from her back-off mantra of last night. Asking Cara to assist with this mock wedding might go down as the best idea he'd had all week.

"Yeah?" he growled, mindful of the eyes on them. "We'll see about that."

His warning was all for show. He didn't mind one bit being at the mercy of the windblown, in-command woman by his side.

She winked and ran through a host of instructions directed at other people while Keith made more mental notes. Cara had done a great job, but nothing was ever perfect. Tweaks could and would be made constantly, even after the resort opened.

Behind them, the music abruptly cut off and the crash of waves filled the silence. Gulls dived overhead, their cries a strange but fitting complement to the scene.

The chef, whose name tag said Hans in an amusing contrast to his clear island heritage, cleared his throat. "Dearly beloved, we are gathered here today to celebrate the—"

"You can skip all that," Keith commented drily. "I do. She does. No one objects."

Cara elbowed him in the ribs. "I'm in charge here and I told him to do the whole spiel. It's not worth practicing if you skip parts. How long will the mock wedding take? Do you know? No. So shut up and listen to the vows like you wrote them yourself."

The crowd muttered their agreement so he took a cue and closed his mouth. She was right, after all.

Hans started again, droning through the ceremony verbiage, and Keith shot Cara a sidelong glance. Under his breath, he whispered, "Careful what you wish for, sweetheart."

"What's that supposed to mean?" she murmured back, and the wind blew a lock of her honey-colored hair across her lips, drawing his gaze.

It meant that he was not one to let a prime opportunity pass to take full advantage of her advice.

"Only that I'm totally on board with not skipping one single part of this ceremony." Keith waited until Hans pronounced them husband and wife and spun Cara into his arms. "Not one."

With deliberate care, he brushed the hair from her lips and replaced it with his mouth. Slowly, to give her time to get used to the idea.

Her body aligned with his and it was like a sledgehammer to the gut. Desire exploded, racing through his veins, heating his skin. It had always been hot with Cara. But not like this, out of control with fast-burning lust.

I want you, right here, right now.

Forget slow. He tightened his arms and tilted his head to find a sweeter angle. Instantly, the kiss deepened into something better suited for behind closed doors. But he couldn't stop.

She softened under his lips, so responsive that he nearly

took her to the sand so he could properly explore every inch of her. Yeah, he'd done that plenty in the past, but not with this Cara, whom he could not get enough of. New discoveries lay just out of reach and the clothes between them needed to be gone.

What had started as a way to get her into his arms without protest had boomeranged on him, detonating into a wild inferno of need.

The hoots and whistles of the crowd registered a moment later.

Cara broke away and his hands fell from her hair, which was slightly mussed from his fingers. That was as sexy as her kissing him back.

What had happened to no distractions?

Cara Chandler-Harris had happened.

Without looking at him again, Cara clapped once to get everyone's attention and reeled off another set of instructions, including a pointed reminder to Mary that she should document every step for the real thing. Cara's wits clearly hadn't been as affected by that kiss as his—he was still in a fuzzy la-la land.

He eyed Cara through the lens of a man who had just kissed a woman and wanted more. "You did a fantastic job with this run-through today. Would you shoot me if I asked for another favor?"

"Depends on what it is."

There it was. Her gaze finally reflected a bit of the unsettled ripples in his own stomach. It cheered him for some strange reason and had him reevaluating how many bruises his ego could actually take.

"Check out the honeymoon suite with me."

She'd either deck him or laugh. He knew it was too soon after the aborted kiss to try again, but with "challenge" practically tattooed across her forehead, he couldn't let it lie.

Plus, he wanted to find out what else might be different from the first time around, because he'd bet anything the changes in Cara went well below surface level.

She didn't blink. "Yes. I'd shoot you if you ask me for that favor. Try again."

He grinned. "Come on. You said it was going to feel very real after the ceremony was over. That kiss was genuine, grade-A attraction between two consenting adults. Let's get real, Cara. Real naked."

At that, she did laugh as he'd predicted, and it warmed him dangerously.

"You've got an expo to organize and I've got dresses to alter so I can launch my designs into the big leagues. That's as real as it's going to get between us. For now."

With that enigmatic parting comment, she sailed toward the main building, leaving Keith to wonder if she'd developed a fondness for playing hard to get.

The first time, he'd pursued her pretty fiercely but she'd proved easy to catch. Had that decreased her attractiveness back then more than he'd credited? Because he couldn't deny he wanted her ten times more now than he had two years ago.

And neither could he deny he'd thoroughly compromised his ability to stay focused on this job. The faster he got Cara into bed, the faster he could burn off this blinding need to figure her out. She was one target he refused to miss.

Five

Rain began pelting the window shortly after Cara escaped to her room. The drops hit the screen with an unsatisfying thud, a distinct contrast from the rhythmic showers of Houston.

She wished she'd never heard of Regent's bridal expo. If she hadn't, she'd still be holed up in her condo, blissfully unaware Keith could still knock down her defenses and blessedly certain she'd fill the yawning chasm inside with a career until she could do a relationship again.

Her lips stung from being kissed by Voldemort Mitchell, who was every inch a wizard of seduction. But the real pain crawled through her chest, and she'd had enough of that for a lifetime. Keith equaled heartbreak. Period.

Why hadn't she slapped him silly? She'd known instantly what he meant by not skipping parts, and even if she hadn't caught the drift, the heated vibe shooting in her direction had been obvious. Every second she wasted on Keith was another second she couldn't get back.

Meredith spilled into the room, laughing. She was drenched down to her underwear, evident by the outline of her bra under her blouse. It had probably been by design—Meredith had never met an exhibitionist tendency she didn't like.

Water pooled under her ruined Pradas as she squeezed out her hair. Cara frowned. Scratch that; they were *Cara's* ruined Pradas.

"When did I tell you that you could borrow my shoes?"

Meredith scrunched up her face as if attempting to recall. "When you were born? It's a sister rule. What's yours is mine and what's mine is mine, remember?"

"Whatever. Ask next time."

"As if you'd have said no or something?" She eased off the shoes and shed her wet clothes as she strode to the bathroom, unconcerned, evidently, about spreading water into the rest of the room. "And stop taking your bad mood out on me. It's not my fault you still have a thing for Keith and he's impossible to escape on a tiny little resort property."

Cara made a face at Meredith's back. "That's not why I'm in a bad mood."

The door to the bathroom shut midsentence, before Cara could insist the real problem was that she'd spent so much time helping Keith today, they were behind on alterations. The hope of gaining national attention for Cara Chandler-Harris Designs was the only thing that made being in this situation with Keith bearable. Her company was like her family and she refused to let them all down because she couldn't stop being attracted to the wrong man.

No matter. Meredith would pick up on the lie. Oh, the alterations were definitely behind, but Cara's current black mood had more to do with the unsettling realization that she hadn't slapped Keith because she'd wanted him to kiss her. The mock wedding had been fun to organize, and she'd gotten caught up in the moment. Who could resist a wedding and Keith and the ocean breeze, all wrapped up in one romantic package?

Except it wasn't her wedding and she wasn't marrying Keith. Just like the last time.

Cara stabbed a needle through the dress in front of her but couldn't get into the right spirit for alterations to wedding dresses. Once again, she'd wear one and still be single when she took it off.

But in stark contrast to last time, she *would* have a thriving business. These alterations represented something greater than the required steps before a model wore the dress down a runway—Cara had a real and lasting place to belong, which this expo was an integral part of promoting.

That was better than a wedding of her own any day. Mostly.

When Meredith exited the bathroom after the longest shower on record, she had her phone in hand. "Paolo just texted me that everyone's in the Caribbean Lounge blowing off steam. Hans threw together a buffet and Keith unlocked the liquor cabinet. Get dressed and come on."

"I'm busy." It was a little too soon to be in Keith's orbit again, especially while in the same galaxy as the rest of the staff, who'd witnessed the scorching kiss their boss had laid on her. The embarrassment over falling so heavily into the playacting hadn't quite faded yet.

"No, you're in sore need of fun, alcohol and sex. All three are within your reach, honey." Meredith slipped into a skin-colored dress that hit her midthigh and made her look as if she should be on the arm of a Grammy-nominee as he walked the red carpet. "Or you can just come eat. You can sulk later. Don't make me go by myself."

"There's zero danger of you being by yourself in that dress."

Her sister shot a treacherous smile over her shoulder. "I

brought that Balenciaga dress that you like. I'll let you wear it, even though you were so mean about the shoes earlier."

Cara's heart twisted. Meredith was a good sister and all Cara had done was snipe at her. Besides, Meredith had been oh so correct—it wasn't her fault Keith and Cara weren't a good mix. "Thanks. I'll come with you. And wear the dress."

The smirk on Meredith's face didn't faze her. Cara was used to letting her sister get her way. In their relationship, that's what love looked like.

The rain hadn't let up and it took a while to get across the resort while sharing a very small umbrella. By the time the sisters arrived, the party was in full swing.

As promised, it did indeed seem as if everyone had come. Mary sat at a four-top laughing with a few of the maids, and Holly, who still looked like a runway model even when off the clock, chatted with the services manager at a mahogany bar near the far wall.

Paolo bounded over, muscles rippling underneath a skin-tight shirt, with two drinks in hand. He handed one to Meredith with an apologetic glance at Cara's empty hand. No big deal. Cara didn't need a pool boy to bring her a drink.

Her sister sipped the frothy pink concoction and smiled the smile she used to humor people. "Thanks, I adore Cosmopolitans."

Martinis, the drier the better, were Meredith's vice of choice. She hadn't touched a drink with an umbrella since a weekend in Vegas that Meredith still refused to talk about.

"For you."

Cara whirled to face the speaker and there was he-who-must-not-be-named himself, holding a wineglass full of deep red liquid. She accepted the goblet from Keith with a nod of thanks, because her stupid heart had just tangled up her tongue too much to talk, and sipped.

God, it was an exquisite cab that swirled through her mouth like a taste of heaven.

"You're serving this to guests?" she asked when she'd stopped worshipping the wine long enough to speak. This was high-quality, exorbitantly expensive stuff, which he no doubt knew that she'd recognize.

"Only the ones in the honeymoon suite." He clinked his glass to hers. "I tried to tell you you'd appreciate checking it out with me, but your mind went straight to the gutter. Shame."

"Yeah, but I still got a glass, so..." She swallowed some more to see if it cooled her suddenly hot throat.

She hadn't *really* been jealous of Meredith's uncomplicated fling with Paolo. Not a whole lot anyway. But all at once, it seemed as though Cara might have the better deal. There was something to be said for having the attention of a man who noticed details, and Keith rarely missed one.

Maybe she should thank Meredith for goading her into joining the party instead of sulking in her room—as her sister put it—which hadn't been too far off. And sulking for what? Because a yummy man kissed her? It was time to relax and stop worrying so much about Keith messing up her plans.

The entertainment director clapped his hands and drew everyone's attention. As he was unfortunately named Mark, someone had apparently thought it appropriate to make him a paper crown with the word *Hurricane* written on it and then crossed out with a large X.

"What's that about?" Cara whispered to Keith. "Is the tropical storm the reason it's raining?"

She hadn't seen a weather report lately, but foreboding gripped her all at once. The expo couldn't go on if the storm hit the island. Could it?

Keith leaned in and his breath teased her hair, sending a quick tug through her middle. She squashed it flat. She'd gone a long time without male companionship—why was she all of a sudden having heated flashes just because a man pressed up against her?

"Why don't you let me worry about the storm?" he suggested, his voice low and sexy in her ear. "I would tell you if there was a problem."

Mark lifted the microphone from its stand. "I need some volunteers to play the resort's version of the *Newlywed Game*. Two couples. Come on down. You don't have to be a real couple, just willing to play."

Cara shot Keith a don't-you-dare look, which he intercepted with a grin. "I wouldn't dream of it. Let some of the others have a chance to pretend to be married."

Keith sank into a chair and patted the one next to him. Since he'd agreed to keep his volunteering mouth shut—and then sweetened the deal by holding up the half-empty bottle of wine—Cara settled into the front-row seat he'd designated for her.

He inclined his head, nose nearly buried in Cara's hair again. "That dress looks amazing on you, by the way."

Cara's cheeks sparked with heat and she wished she could claim it was the only hot spot on her body. "Go on. You say that to all the girls."

"You're the only one I'm talking to. Which is not an accident."

He slung an arm across the back of her chair as if this was a date or something and she thought long and hard about staring at him with disapproval until he removed it. But the borrowed dress had a low back, and Keith's sleeve brushed her skin pleasantly. It would probably draw a lot of attention if she made a big deal out of it. So she leaned against his arm and ignored all the heat being generated by his close proximity.

To the surprise of no one, Meredith and Paolo lined up on the small stage at the front of the lounge and took the seats Mark had set up on the left-hand side. Cecelia, one of the maids, and the baby-faced kid who had set up chairs for Cara on the beach hopped up on stage to take the other set of chairs.

Mark handed out dry erase tablets and markers to all the "newlyweds" and asked the wives to answer the first question about their new husbands. "Boxers or briefs?"

The contestants scrawled their answers and when Mark said "Reveal!" the wives flipped their tablets. Cara rolled her eyes at Meredith's board, which read "Neither" in flowery script with a heart over the *i*.

Paolo's dimples popped out as he flipped his board. It read "Nada."

The crowd clapped and laughed simultaneously. Cecelia and her baby-faced fake husband, who apparently weren't on intimate terms, had opposite answers, so Meredith and Paolo got a point.

"I'm surprised you allowed everyone a break," Cara murmured to Keith, tilting her head close, mostly so he could hear her over the crowd noise, but it wasn't a chore to inhale his masculine scent at the same time.

"It's hard to crack the whip twenty-four/seven when everyone's worked like dogs for days and days," Keith allowed. "We can get back to the grind tomorrow, assuming we can find enough indoor tasks to keep us busy."

It was an unexpected admission from someone like Keith, who thought the sun rose and set over the bottom line, but she covered her shock. "That's very humane of you."

Her sister and the pool boy continued to dominate and won handily, high-fiving each other as Mark pronounced them the champions. Meredith and Paolo strutted across the stage, lording their victory over the poor fake couple who clearly knew each other only in passing.

Cara, meanwhile, had drained her wineglass and for God

knew what insane reason, yelled out, "Bet you couldn't beat a real couple."

Her sister threw a glance over her shoulder. "Bet there's not one in this room. Therefore, we are champions, my friends." Meredith devolved into an obnoxious Queen number, karaoke-style, complete with upraised fingers in the classic V for Victory.

That was the last straw.

"Come on." Cara didn't even glance at Keith before she grabbed his hand and hauled him up on stage. To Meredith, she simply said, "You're going down, honey."

Thankfully, Keith hadn't protested Cara's impulsive move or she'd have looked really silly trying to drag him someplace he didn't want to go.

"You think?" Her sister smiled as if she had the secret address to a 50-percent-off sale on designer shoes. "Sit down, Paolo. Let's show them how it's done."

The crowd hooted their approval and Mark fished around for a second set of questions.

Cara risked a glance at Keith, who was watching her with amusement. "What?" she asked defensively.

"Thought you weren't interested in pretending to be a couple."

"I'm not pretending. We've seen each other naked. Should be a snap to kick the behind of the—" Cara stuck two fingers of each hand in the air to make air quotes "—champions."

"So you're not going to be happy with me if we lose, are you?"

"No. So don't lose," she advised.

With a verbal drumroll, Mark asked the first question of the wives. "What's your favorite position?"

Cara winced. Okay, she'd totally deserved that. She shook her head and wrote, "Missionary," because it was true, thank God.

Mama would have heart palpitations if she knew her daughter was flaunting her sexual preferences for an audience, but at least Cara could maintain *some* dignity.

"Reveal!" Mark yelled.

Meredith and Cara flipped their boards. The crowd laughed and Cara craned her neck to see Meredith's, which read "CEO."

Cara bit back a smile. Meredith had enough ambition to decide what to eat for dinner that night, but definitely not enough to become CEO of anything. Her sister was letting her win, the big dolt, as a peace offering for bullying Cara into coming to the bar.

Keith flipped his board, and it thankfully read "Missionary."

Paolo's board read "All of them," so Keith and Cara received the point.

Except she hardly noticed because she was picturing Keith poised over her, every inch of his delicious body bared. The things that man could do to her—

Keith cleared his throat and she blinked at him, fairly certain the wicked glint in his eye meant he knew exactly what she'd been fantasizing about. And he heartily approved.

Heat rolled over her and she squirmed against the hard chair as she envisioned what might happen if she agreed to test the honeymoon suite after the party. As a bonus, the suite might have another bottle of that awesome wine.

No. No naked after-party honeymoon suites. She was here to work, not waste time and energy on an island fling with a man who'd already had a chance to "fling" with her all he wanted and instead chose to let her watch his backside as it disappeared.

"Next question," Mark said. "Few people know this about your husband, but he's… Okay, wives, fill in the blank!"

Oh, God. What kind of question was *that*? Cara scoured her memory but came up with exactly nothing. Meredith had already scribbled down her answer, so Cara wrote the only thing that might work, and revealed her board.

It read: "A jogger." At least it was true.

But Keith had written down "A microbrewer."

"What does that even mean?" Cara demanded, too surprised to do it quietly. "A microbrewer? Of beer?"

Keith shrugged. "It's been my hobby for ten years."

Yeah, she got the not-so-subtle dig. Keith had been making his own beer throughout the period they'd been a couple. And she'd been totally oblivious.

This game was stupid. But that didn't eliminate the panicky twinge in her midsection.

Their competition had both written "Third-degree black belt" for the point. Really? Cara eyed Paolo with new respect and squashed the odd feeling that her sister knew her Caribbean fling better than Cara knew the man she'd almost married.

The next question had Cara scouting for her wineglass. "My husband and I are complete opposites when it comes to _____."

Somehow, she suspected *marriage* wouldn't go over well as an answer to a newlywed game. The last of the amazing cab went down smoothly but didn't jog her brain. What was with all these fill-in-the-blank questions? At least Mark could have supplied some choices. These questions were much harder than the ones he'd asked in the first round.

Harder, because she and Keith were virtually strangers now. Maybe they always had been. After all, she hadn't even known about his aversion to commitment until recently. *Before* she'd planned a wedding might have been a better time to learn that.

When would it have been a good time to find out he wasn't in love with her? Better yet, shouldn't she have realized that on her own? But she hadn't even realized her own feelings weren't as strong as she'd told herself. She'd have sworn she was in love with Keith, but how could she have been? She couldn't even name his hobby.

In desperation, Cara wrote "Religion." Keith was Catholic and Cara had gone to a Methodist church growing up. It was the only thing she could think of.

Keith's board said "Balancing our checkbook."

"Oh, for heaven's sake. I've told you a million times that I *do* balance my checkbook." Cara threw up her hands. "When I get my monthly statement, I enter all the transactions in my checkbook and voilà. It balances."

Or at least that was how she'd done it before, when her father subsidized the account. Now she watched every dime, but Keith didn't have to know that.

"That how you run your business, too?" he asked mildly.

"Please." Cara snorted. "I pay a CPA to deal with all of that."

With a deadpan expression, Keith tapped the board. "Like I said. Complete opposites."

Opposites in everything else important, too, like marriage, children and love. The thought rang a little false, especially since she was beginning to realize she didn't have a firm grip on all those things either. Was that why she couldn't seem to get past the wedding and become an actual wife?

"We mere mortals can't add up the contents of a full shopping cart in our heads." Cara waved a hand to encompass the rapt crowd. "Well, we can, but we wouldn't be within a few pennies like you, Mitchell."

His smile could have melted butter. "I'll take that as a compliment, both that you recall something as mundane as grocery shopping together and that you've bestowed divine status on me. Guess we *are* complete opposites when it comes to religion."

Lord Voldemort had spoken. She chuckled darkly, though at what, she had no idea.

Mark clapped his hands, oblivious to the rising tension. Cara's spine hurt from holding it so straight, but she couldn't relax.

"Last question," the emcee shouted. "Who was the first person to say 'I love you'?"

Cara's board dropped to the floor with a crash. She couldn't do this particular brand of torture anymore.

Keith smiled apologetically at his staff and followed Cara's flight from the lounge. He only hoped that she wouldn't take out his kneecaps when he caught up with her.

But he couldn't let her go, not when it was obvious how close to tears she was. This wasn't a little snit because they were losing, but something else entirely. And he had an unexplainable urge to know what had provoked her.

If it was the checkbook joke, she really needed to lighten up.

Cara dashed through the rain, surprisingly swift for someone wearing heels in a downpour. Finally, she reached the door of her room and ducked inside. Keith bolted for the threshold and put a palm to the door before she could slam it in his face. To be fair, she probably didn't realize he'd been behind her.

He eased into the room, fully prepared to be thrown out, but determined to at least make sure she was okay before leaving. "Hey."

Cara whirled. "What do you want?"

The sight of a drenched Cara punched him—hard—in the gut. Her little pink dress was plastered to her body as if it had been painted on, and she'd clearly forgotten that she wasn't wearing a bra. Tight, hard nipples poked the fabric, and it was far more erotic than if she'd stood before him completely nude. Her hair hung in damp hanks around her face as if placed there by a team of designers for the maximum sexiest effect.

"You okay?" he managed to choke out.

She wiped her eyes with the back of her hand. "Obviously not. I left because I wanted to be alone. Go away."

"Sure thing." Keith crossed his arms and leaned against the door frame. There was no way he was leaving now, not while she was still upset. And definitely not while the view was so wet and so smoking hot. "As soon as you tell me what's up. I've never known you to be so competitive as to get mad over being beaten."

"Well, that's the problem, isn't it?" she shot back, her voice wobbly and clogged with baffling undercurrents. "You don't really know me that well, do you?"

"Not nearly as well as I'd like," he admitted readily. "Hence the invitation to join me in the honeymoon suite."

She rolled her shiny eyes, and the moisture wasn't from the storm overhead, but the internal one. "You already know me that way, Mitchell."

"Do I?" Any sensible person would shut the door. It *was* raining. So he eased it closed and leaned back against it. "You haven't developed some new moves under the sheets in two years? You've started jogging. Maybe you're doing some tantric yoga, too."

Fire flashed in her gaze and all the tears dried up, which was exactly what he'd been going for. All her unexplained emotions were unsettling. Uncomfortable. Sweat broke out along his neck.

"I'm not. And for your information, I've been building a business for the last two years, not brushing up on my *Kama Sutra*." She raked him with that fiery gaze. "So what if you get me naked and it's cataclysmic. What then? What does that really tell you about me—as a person?"

"That you're someone I want to spend more time with?" he offered and pulled at his tight shirt. She was clearly fishing for something. "And God, Cara. It's like an oven in here. How do you sleep?"

"Yeah, the air conditioner is still broken. Thanks for noticing." Her sarcasm only made the neckline of his shirt more constricting. "Don't you dare use that as an excuse to try to get me into your bed."

"I wouldn't dream of it," he lied. She didn't have to know that was exactly what he'd been about to suggest.

Still off balance, Keith ran a hand through his own damp hair. He kind of hoped the fantasy in pink never figured out she looked like a model about to pose for the cover of a men's magazine—but she was killing him. In more ways than one.

He should leave. Tension crackled through the air and he only wished it was just sexual. That he could handle. But the sizzling awareness was laced with something heavy, deeper. And he wasn't sure what to do with it, not on the heels of the mind-bending kiss on the beach. Not on the heels of playing the newlywed game and recalling Cara underneath him with extreme clarity.

He glanced at the wall behind her, but it did nothing to ease the churn of warring responses beneath his skin. Maybe they should get back to the original subject.

"What's going on with you? If you took off because Meredith and her stud boy were winning, I wouldn't put too much credence into it. The only reason she knew Paolo was a black belt is because he uses that as a pickup line. He's told every available woman on this property that he's a black belt. Whether he actually is or not is another story."

The wall was a very boring beige with a framed photo of a shell hanging dead center. Who decorated these rooms— a half-blind eighty-year-old? The decor would have to be updated. Yet another detail he'd missed with his fine-toothed comb because he was too busy chasing after a woman who'd already rejected him countless times over the past couple days.

His gaze drifted to Cara's face. Who was he kidding? He couldn't stop looking at her any more than he could stop digging beneath the surface of her "not interested." Any more than he could stop wanting her.

"I didn't know he was a black belt." Cara sniffed, but her expression lost a bit of the edge she'd worn since he walked into her room.

"You're not available," he pointed out. "Are you?"

"No! Well, maybe. I don't know." She dropped onto the bed as if her legs couldn't hold her any longer and scrubbed at her cheeks with her palms. "That's what's wrong. I don't know anymore."

Defeat pulled at her expression and another unsettling wave splashed through his insides.

Talk to me, sweetheart. He wanted to say it. Meant to say it.

But he couldn't spit out the words.

Cara fingered off her sandals and while she was occupied, Keith risked sitting on the bed next to her. Bad move. Now he was close enough to touch the fantasy in pink and very far from the door, which he should be disappearing through at this moment.

Especially given that he'd just looked down from this emotionally precarious tightrope and nearly lost his balance.

She needed…something, and Keith Mitchell was probably the last person on the planet able to give it to her.

For once, he had no idea how to hit this target.

Six

He had to do something, so he reached out and enfolded her hand in his, cradling it in his lap without speaking.

Her fingers curled around his and his stomach settled. Slightly.

"You don't have to stick around and watch me fall apart," she said. "I'm sure there are plenty of other things you'd rather be doing. Go back to the party. I'll be fine."

"There's nothing I'd rather be doing than sitting here with you." Which seemed to be the God's honest truth, despite all the heaviness. Otherwise, he would have taken advantage of his close proximity to the door to make his escape, wouldn't he?

He tried to convince himself he stayed because of the challenge. But he had a feeling there was more to it than that, and the mystery of it kept him firmly rooted.

"Only because you think you're going to get lucky."

"Yeah, that's why I'm here, Cara." Frustration exploded through his chest and came out of his mouth, unchecked.

Anger he didn't have any trouble expressing. "I live to take advantage of crying, upset women. It's a total turn-on. Can you please stop assuming all I care about is sex?"

Clearly stricken, she stared at him. "I'm sorry. I didn't… Wait. You mean that's *not* all you care about?"

Keith groaned. The trap had closed so neatly, he hadn't even realized he'd set it up. And he had only himself to blame. Five minutes ago, sex *was* all he cared about. Or at least it was all he could think about. When had everything shifted around?

It made him mad enough to say exactly what was on his mind.

"Let's examine this, shall we? I'm missing a party where alcohol I'm paying for is flowing freely. It's raining and I followed you back to your room anyway. My pants are still wet." Which he'd totally forgotten about until now, but he was too worked up to recall why it was important to mention. "You're upset and in a crappy mood. I would have assumed the facts speak for themselves, but since they don't, I'll spell it out. I care about you," he said honestly, though who the hell knew where that came from. "Or I wouldn't be here."

"Oh." She processed that, a hundred unfathomable thoughts traveling across her face at warp speed. "I'm sorry I dragged you away from the party. And for being in a crappy mood. It's not your fault, by the way. I'm just questioning every life decision I've ever made and you happened to get caught in the crossfire."

"Good to know. By the way, I'm not here to stand in the way of your crisis. Question away," he offered because it was the closest thing to support he could muster. "I'll listen."

She flung herself backward on the bed, legs still dangling off the edge. Staring at the ceiling as if it held the secrets of the universe, she hefted a sigh. "How did we get all the way to the point where we were about to march down the aisle and didn't really know each other that well?"

"Uh…" *You were pregnant* clearly wasn't what she was going for. "I think the better question is why it matters so much to you. We didn't march down the aisle."

"But I would have. I don't even think I was in love with you. I convinced myself I was. But I don't *know* that I was. How could I not know?" Her fists came down hard on the bed, but it didn't seem to unload an iota of her frustration. The motion flung still-damp hair into her face, but she left it there in favor of cursing colorfully at the ceiling.

"Where is this coming from? The stupid newlywed game? That was supposed to be fun, not an opportunity to ponder the choices we made a million years ago." He couldn't help but reach out and stroke the hair from her forehead since she didn't appear to be so inclined. Plus it was an excuse to touch her…and maybe communicate something he couldn't with mere words.

"Yeah. From the game. But also from the elevator conversation. The kiss." She bit her lip. "Never mind. Scratch that last one."

His hand froze against her temple. "Not on your life. What about the kiss?"

She hesitated long enough for him to assume she wasn't going to answer. But then she rolled to face him, effectively threading his fingers through her hair. "It was just… different. I've kissed you before. Lots of times. How could it be different?"

Before he answered that, he needed a critical piece of intel. "Different better or different worse?"

"Fishing for compliments?" At his eye roll, she shrugged with a faint smile. "It wasn't worse. But it wasn't like it used to be."

That might be the best news he'd heard all day. Satisfaction flared to life and turned dangerously fast into an ache in his chest that couldn't be explained. "Maybe because it was spontaneous, without all the pressures we had the first time around?"

"Maybe."

Stroking her temple some more because he liked it and because he could, he weighed what he wanted to say versus what she probably needed to hear. This was important and he didn't want to flub it up.

"We got serious really fast. And we're at different places in our lives now. You're a business owner. I took on the biggest consulting gig of my career and it came with hefty responsibilities." Grasping at straws and totally out of his depth, he took a stab at helping her make sense of things. "Neither of us really has the luxury of a permanent relationship, and the kiss was about nothing more than being in the moment."

No. It hadn't been. That was so far from the truth, he should take it back immediately. That kiss had been about need. About exploring what had changed, what was exciting about who they were now.

Deny it, Cara. Tell me it meant something.

"That's the problem." Her mouth turned down. "A relationship is what I want. Or I did. Now I don't think I do."

"What do you want?" He was clearly so bad at this, so bad at reading her, he should win a Terrible Person in a Crisis award.

"My whole life I've wanted to have a big wedding and be blissfully happy as Mrs. Someone. And then you left." She speared him through the heart with a baleful glance and went on without even giving him an opportunity to counter the offense. "I told myself no more pining for what obviously isn't meant to be and put my head down to make something of Cara Chandler-Harris Designs. When I looked up, I had a wedding dress business instead of a husband.

And that's probably what should have happened. During the last few days, I realized I don't even know what love is."

Misery pulled at her expression, dampening her eyes, and it was so painful, Keith cupped her face with his palms, forcing her to look at him. "Who does? You think Meredith and Paolo are in love and that's why she knows the answers to a few inane questions? Love isn't all it's cracked up to be."

Love probably didn't even exist. It had never touched his existence in any form or fashion. But the greeting card industry would have the entire world believing in it if it had its way. So what did he know?

"Obviously." She made a face. "It's just hard. I thought I was trying to get over you, and instead I got a great big wake-up call that I have no idea what a relationship should be. Now what am I supposed to do?"

"Sounds like you need a hot and heavy tropical island fling with someone who knows how to treat you right," he suggested with an eyebrow lift. "No pressure. No wedding bells in the future. It would be nothing but two consenting adults having some fun."

Which was not so coincidentally what he needed, too, more than he could possibly explain to her. Or himself. That's why he preferred to keep things temporary and easy—because he wasn't good at anything else.

"That would be great, except Paolo seems pretty happy with my sister."

"Ouch." It took every ounce of his considerable stamina to utter that one word without sounding pathetic.

She eyed him. "I'll take your words of wisdom under advisement, okay? Thanks for hanging out with me, but I'm beat and I just need to shut my eyes in a tomorrow-is-another-day kind of thing."

He'd been dismissed. Soundly. "Get some sleep. I'll be around."

Keith let himself out and cursed the fates that had seen fit to strand him on an island with a woman he wanted more than his next breath but couldn't seem to get naked.

Somehow he'd managed to have an emotionally charged conversation and gotten through it without having a heart attack. And he had the distinct impression he'd also managed to give Cara the support she'd needed without taking a thing for himself.

What was she *doing* to him?

He dashed through the rain to the other building and went to his room instead of back to the party. He preferred being alone anyway, didn't he?

When Cara opened her eyes, she was shocked to note the clock read 7:00 a.m.

The lump in the next bed had appeared sometime during the night. Cara hadn't even heard Meredith come in. Either her sister had learned to enter a hotel room at something less than the force of a tornado, or Cara had been more exhausted than she'd realized. She'd slept the whole night through without waking once.

After the kiss and Keith being all understanding and strong and spread out over her bed like the best possible thing she could have ordered from room service, she'd been convinced the combination would result in a sleepless night of tossing and turning.

Apparently not.

She rolled from the bed and peeked out the window in the off chance it had stopped raining. It hadn't. She rolled her twinging ankle. Not too sore today. Maybe it would be fun to jog on the beach in the rain. At least the odds of running into Keith were slim.

She was still downhearted to discover all her hopes and dreams were twisted up. And she had no crystal ball to help her sort out what her real goals were. What they should be. Keith would only make her confusion worse.

He met up with her ten yards outside her door.

"Run with me?" he asked casually as if everything was cool between them.

And really, wasn't it? As he'd said, neither of them was in a good place for a relationship. He knew she was an emotional mess and hadn't fled screaming into the night. Nor had he tried to take advantage of her while she'd been conflicted and upset.

The invitation to slide beneath the sheets with him had been quite clear. But he'd never pressed her, choosing to let the invitation stand without being obnoxious about it.

Keith had been very gentlemanly last night, all things considered. He deserved a break.

"Sure. I'd like to run with you."

To his credit, he didn't make a wisecrack.

They ran in silence through the downpour. The wet sand proved a little more treacherous than Cara had expected so she concentrated on fighting the elements instead of worrying about the mistakes of the past or the nebulous future.

It was a downright therapeutic experience.

After two miles down the beach and two miles back, they slowed near the bridal bower where they'd promised to love, honor and cherish in the fake wedding.

"What's on your agenda for today?" Cara asked, suddenly reluctant to end what had been a nice way to start the day. Rain notwithstanding.

And to be honest, she couldn't get last night's conversation out of her mind. If he wasn't interested only in sex, what *was* he interested in?

"I'm personally inspecting each hotel room. If yours is any indication, they're not ready for public consumption, and the majority of the guests are due tomorrow for the start of the expo."

"That's a big task, isn't it?" There had to be over five hundred rooms on the resort grounds, and her building still didn't have a working elevator.

He smiled slightly. "All my tasks are huge. Staving off Tropical Storm Mark being the insurmountable one."

She'd been trying to convince herself the rain was normal for this time of year and nothing to worry about, but something about his tone struck her. "We're going to get hit, aren't we?"

Keith swiped rain off his face in a deliberate gesture. "I think you should revise that to present tense instead of future."

The sound of dismay rose up in Cara's throat before she could stop it. "What? Can we weather the storm here on the island? I mean, is it safe?"

Lord above, they were on an island during a tropical storm. Every hurricane documentary she'd ever watched on the Weather Channel flashed through her mind in full color, including what 120-mile-an-hour winds could do to a building, not to mention the flooding.

Why hadn't they evacuated the island when there was still a chance of getting out?

"Safer than the rickety huts the island residents live in. The brunt of the storm is still a hundred miles away and may still miss us in the end. We should be fine here on the west side of the island. Maybe we'll lose power for a few hours." He shrugged. "The show must go on."

He seemed nonchalant about it, so Cara tried to relax. After all, he was the one with the NOAA app. There must not be imminent danger, right? She chewed on a fingernail and immediately yanked it out of her mouth. Destroying her manicure would not cause the storm to veer away. She'd have to find another way to de-stress.

"Let me help you inspect the rooms," she volunteered impulsively.

There was no way Cara could sit around and nervously wait to be battered by a tropical storm. Meredith could stay in the hotel room and do alterations all day if the weather was only going to get worse.

He eyeballed her. "Don't you have stuff to do?"

"Yeah, but I'm the boss." She liked the sound of that. It was the first time she'd ever thought of herself as such. But when you signed all the checks, what other title could you give yourself? "That means I can order my lackeys to do the work while I…go do other work."

"I'll take all the help I can get, then. Meet me in the lobby in forty-five minutes?"

"Sure." Plenty of time. It wasn't as if she planned to get all dressed up to tramp around in the rain. She might not even take a shower.

She ended up just changing clothes and shoving a packaged muffin into her mouth for breakfast. Her sister groused about being forced to do slave labor while Cara jetted off to hang out with Keith and then drank her coffee with a sulky pout. But by the time Cara was ready to leave, Meredith had a sewing kit in her hand.

Cara hid a smile. The reason her design business had grown so successful so fast was because she genuinely valued the place she'd created for herself—and the other girls in her employ. Meredith included. It was the best kind of pseudo-family because they'd all chosen to be in it.

"I'll be back later," Cara said and ducked back out into the rain, where she thoroughly squashed the little voice inside that was asking what in the hell she thought she was doing running off and leaving both her family and her responsibilities. And for what? To help Keith *work*?

Keith flashed a smile when he caught sight of her walking toward him in the lobby. Her borrowed flip-flops squeaked on the marble tile, but he didn't even glance down. He kept his attention squarely on her face, and that killer smile lit up her insides. She sighed. Maybe her impulsive offer was a veiled attempt to hang out in Keith's presence in hopes he'd give her a little more insight into his thoughts. There wasn't a law against it.

She'd almost married him but hardly understood his basic motivations. It was far past time to change that.

He handed her an electronic tablet.

"What's this?" She glanced at it. Holy cow, the screen displayed a fifty-item-long checklist.

"Each room has to pass with at least forty-eight of these, but none of the problems can be in the top ten." Keith tapped the screen. "Only 100 percent in the top ten will do. As you inspect a room, enter the room number at the top and then use the stylus to hit the check box for each item."

"This is very...involved." It would take an hour to inspect one room. Maybe instead of running herself ragged doing a job she really didn't have time for, she should just admit she wanted to get to know the Keith Mitchell from last night. Who he'd been. Who he was now. What he hoped for the future.

"Regent hired me to turn this resort around. Rooms were rated the lowest for the last five years on customer surveys."

"You should have at least ten people doing this job if you plan to finish today."

"That's probably true. But I don't trust anyone else to meet my high standards."

Yet he trusted her. Her insides exploded with warmth and she was pathetically grateful to have signed up for this exhausting task. "Where should we start?"

He pointed upward, eyes on his own tablet as he tapped a few times. "This tower. We'll go to the top floor and work our way down, you on one side of the hall, me on the other."

Though she didn't have a very clear picture of what she'd intended this morning's activities to look like, that sounded like the exact opposite of it. "You mean we're inspecting separately? I thought we'd do it together."

The taps stopped abruptly and Keith's gaze swung up to meet hers, the caramel in his eyes wickedly decadent. "You do realize we're inspecting hotel rooms. Empty rooms. With beds. Right?"

Answering heat rose up in her middle, flushing outward. "Of course I realize that. Are you worried I'll take advantage of you, sugar? I'll keep my hands to myself."

She *so* shouldn't be flirting with him. It was dangerous and would give him the wrong idea. Unfortunately, she wasn't sure any longer what idea was the right one.

He chuckled and it rolled through her. "We'll get this task completed much faster if you're in a totally separate room, trust me."

They worked on their respective rooms for an hour or two until Cara thought she could do the whole process in her sleep. Art on the walls. Check. Shower curtain present and accounted for. Check. Air conditioner operational. Check.

That one hurt. Every room so far had a functional air conditioner. By the twentieth room, she had a bone to pick with the man in charge around here. Plus, doing all of this alone was boring.

"What's the deal, Mitchell?" she demanded as she poked her head into the last room she'd seen him disappear into. Not that she'd paid attention or anything.

Keith exited the bathroom, tablet in hand, and good gravy—the man exuded something she couldn't tear her gaze from. He'd shed his suit jacket and rolled up the sleeves on his button-down shirt, letting sinewy forearms speak to what the rest of his body looked like.

"The deal about what?" he asked.

Her mood veered into dangerous territory. Keith was not part of the plan. Wanting him was not part of the plan.

Of course, the biggest problem was she had no plan. And confusion was not something she did well.

"All of these rooms have air conditioners. How come I'm staying in the one room on the whole property where it's broken?"

"If I recall, you told me not to use that as an excuse to get you into my bed." He crossed his arms, tucking the tablet under one. "I didn't."

"Move me to one of these rooms." She mirrored his stance and leaned a shoulder against the door frame, prepared to be as obstinate as Keith until the cows came home. "This one looks good."

"These rooms are all intended for expo guests. I can't put them in the tower with the broken elevator."

She scowled. "But it's okay for the help to be in the other tower?"

His quick grin put a flutter in her tummy. And that was not cool.

"You won't write an article about the elevator or lack of air-conditioning in a bridal magazine. I need the guests to be wowed. You will accomplish that with amazing wedding dresses. I will accomplish that by ensuring every last one of these rooms is up to par for the VIPs arriving tomorrow."

Somehow she'd crossed the threshold and met Keith in the middle. "*Your* room is in this tower."

"Yep." He slid a sizzling once-over down the length of her body and the unspoken message was pretty clear—he would gladly share his room with her, but it was the only one available in this tower. And she'd already declined.

Without checking her strength, she poked a finger in the middle of his chest. "Stop being so logical."

God, he was so tall when she wasn't wearing heels. And the chest under her finger was hard with well-defined muscles she remembered well. It took an enormous amount of will to keep the pad of her finger in one place instead of tracing the plane of his torso south until she hit the six-pack abs he surely still had.

Why couldn't she? He wouldn't stop her. In fact, he would probably encourage it.

He glanced down at her finger. "Thought you were keeping your hands to yourself. Did you find something you wanted to touch bad enough to break your self-imposed rule?"

Just as she flexed to snatch back her hand, he captured her palm with his own, holding hers tight against his pectoral and yeah, it was still hard as stone. His heart thudded against her hand, speeding up as she glanced at his lips. They'd felt amazing when he kissed her, and it didn't matter how hard she'd tried to forget, she couldn't.

"It was more of a guideline than an actual rule. Also an example of you being too logical." She should go back to the room she'd been inspecting. The checklist was only about half-complete and…

"Sure you want me to stop being logical?" he asked softly. "Logic has its benefits. For example, we're in a hotel room where a newly married couple will eventually stay. It would be a shame if the bed didn't hold up to a vigorous round of honeymoon sex. Logically, I should ensure this resort gets high marks on all aspects of Regent's destination wedding services."

"That's very um…logical." Apparently her brain had now completely deserted her. Because she definitely didn't want to go anywhere and definitely didn't think it was a good idea to stay.

He dipped his head, lips hovering near hers, then he turned slightly to murmur in her ear in a hot tease. "I'm glad you agree."

His nose nuzzled her ear and through no fault of her own, her head swiveled, causing his lips to collide with her neck. She arched involuntarily at the pleasurable contact.

Never at a loss, he molded his mouth to her skin expertly, finding the perfect hollow to lave. It sent a shower of sparks along her throat, and she moaned.

Seeking fingers gripped her face and he guided her chin toward him. His mouth claimed hers, swallowing her moan, and when his arms snaked around her waist, he hefted her against his solid frame.

Her body ignited. He kissed her with tightly wound control but the hint of abandon was there, just below the surface. He'd let his control drop the moment she said so, and devoured her with carnal pleasure until she cried out under the onslaught.

Yes, this was *definitely* what she'd intended when volunteering for this Herculean task. One telling comment yesterday—*I care about you*—had possibly changed the course of their future.

She wanted to explore it, wanted to find that place she belonged, that place she'd thought she found with him two years ago. What might be possible now that hadn't been back then? In the past few days, she felt as if she'd learned more about Keith than she had in the entire six months they'd been together before. She wanted more, wanted him.

She wanted to know what love looked like—*felt* like— in a relationship. She wanted to know what love felt like in *their* relationship. True love, not the pale shadow of affection they'd held for each other before.

The kiss deepened and Keith drenched her senses with his hard masculine body and powerful, purposeful hands. She inhaled him. He shifted a knee between her legs, and the rough friction sparked at her core. Hot and thick desire billowed over her skin, scorching her from the inside out.

Keith's phone beeped, startling her and effectively breaking the mood. How had she gotten so lost in him so fast? They were both in the middle of the biggest projects of their respective careers and all she could think about was exploring the depths of the man in charge.

Pulling back, she peered up at him. "Do you need to get that?"

"Wasn't planning on it." He made a noise of disgust. "Guess I will now."

She smiled at his consternation. "We can pick this up again later."

His wolfish smile put the exclamation point on it. "That was always going to happen. I was thinking we could pick it up again now *and* later."

Clarity rushed in to fill the space where the saturation of Keith had been a moment ago.

She made a face. "Despite the logic in testing *all* aspects of the room, we both have a lot of work to do today. Besides, if we really wanted to do it right, we'd have to test the bed in every room."

"Funny, I was thinking the same thing." Keith glanced at his phone and spit out the filthiest curse in his vocabulary.

He uttered that word in her presence only when something really bad had happened. "What's going on?"

Seven

Now that Cara had put the brakes on what would have surely turned into a naked free-for-all, Keith was having a hard time getting his body to understand playtime was over.

And over in a big way.

He glanced at the message on his phone again in a poor attempt to reorient. Instead of siphoning the blood from his lower half and returning it to his brain—where it needed to be—all his phone did was infuriate him further. The news hadn't changed.

"Looks like we're inspecting these rooms for no reason," he explained and ungritted his teeth. "Tropical Storm Mark has shut down Providenciales Airport."

As if this project needed another complication.

"What does that mean? The expo is canceled?" Worry crinkled the corners of Cara's eyes.

He'd prefer it if her gaze was still full of come-hither. He blew out his frustration in a heavy sigh and tapped a quick message to Elena, the resort manager, on his phone.

"No way. Well…I don't know. But we have to assume the airport will be reopened in a few hours. And if it is, we have to be prepared for the expo to go on as scheduled."

Which vastly increased his mile-long to-do list. Additional staff members should have arrived today, all of whom had critical roles in preparing for a wide range of expo elements.

Was it five o'clock yet? Hell, the rapid deterioration of Keith's mood and the expo might call for tequila shots in the middle of the day regardless of his rules against drinking on the job.

The interruption and subsequent issues were both nasty reminders that he wasn't on vacation with Cara, free to seduce her into having sex on the beach, skinny-dipping in the hot tub or taking a long shower together. The only water in their future was pouring down from the sky.

It was unsettling to realize he resented the gargantuan pile of tasks standing between him and what he wanted. Turning this resort into a premier wedding destination was his job, and the number of zeroes Regent had tacked on to the end of his paycheck made it well worth his while. But for the first time in his professional life, what he wanted had nothing to do with the job.

Frustrated beyond all belief, he sent another text to Alice, instructing her to call a meeting with the core management team. Everyone would look to him for leadership in the wake of the airport closures and imminent storm, and he couldn't fail them.

"I've got to finish these rooms and then run to a meeting," he said instead of laying Cara on the bed as he'd planned.

Cara picked up her tablet from the dresser where she'd dropped it earlier. "I take it we won't be picking things up later?"

There was no way he'd have time for Cara later—she

deserved more than a fifteen-minute quickie. *He* deserved more than that.

Well, there was one way. According to Cara's philosophy, being the boss meant you could order your employees to do extra work. Perhaps it was time to delegate a few things.

"If I can plow through the most critical issues, I'll text you, maybe around nine. Come to my room and have a drink. Don't be late," he advised.

"Or what?" she shot back.

"Or I'll come looking for you and you will lose one article of clothing for every minute it takes me to find you."

She laughed throatily. "Are you trying to get me there on time or convince me I'd rather be tardy?"

"Go." He pushed her gently in the direction of the door. "Finish the rooms on your side, and for God's sake, let me do mine without you entering any more of your air-conditioner grievances onto the record."

They parted and he didn't stop checking off items on the inspection list until Alice texted him that everyone was in the staff meeting room in the main building. He dashed through the rain, and spent the afternoon having terse conversations about fun concepts like contingency plans, insurance claims and flood preparation.

It took a supreme act of will to remain focused, especially when he'd rather be drowning his sorrows in Cara. Elena ordered food to be brought in at some point and Keith ate without tasting it, one ear on Mary as she talked through ideas for how to move the expo indoors. The remainder of his attention stayed fixed to his computer screen, where a constantly refreshing radar image tracked Mark.

The good news: the tropical storm hadn't been upgraded to a hurricane.

The bad news: it was still a tropical storm and the airport hadn't been reopened.

Alice typed up notes and split the tasks amongst the senior management. Keith's list contained exactly the same number as everyone else's because at the end of the day, he didn't have the heart to foist more work on his staff just because he had a selfish desire to get an old flame between the sheets.

No one left the little meeting room and Keith didn't look up until nearly ten o'clock. Wind howled outside, occasionally gripping solid objects and flinging them against the side of the building. The storm had slowed the moment it hit land and battered the island for hours.

The airport remained closed indefinitely and Keith's doubled workload had decreased by two items in two hours. The long evening loomed, promising to be lonely and stressful, but only because he'd hoped to have other plans. Most days, stress couldn't touch him because he lived and breathed his work and liked it that way.

Elena plopped into the next chair and put her head in her hands, groaning.

"Yeah," Keith commiserated. "Tell me about it."

"It's that definition of insanity. You know, doing the same thing over and over again and expecting different results? I look at the agenda for the expo, and every time I think I'm going to see a magic solution that will allow us to kick it off tomorrow as planned."

"There's no magic. Just hours upon hours of hard work for zero payoff." Normally, he'd sugarcoat a comment like that at least a little bit, but he was out of both sugar and patience.

Elena frowned. "That's unacceptable."

And that was typically Keith's line. An unwillingness to fail coupled with hard-core will got him through the day.

"You're right. There will be a payoff. Eventually." It was just hard to see it right this minute through the red haze of professional and personal roadblocks. "I don't know what's wrong with me."

"You've been putting in twelve- and sixteen-hour days for weeks," Elena said mildly. "Take a break. The storm is going to do what it's going to do and no spreadsheet in existence will change that. Let's reconvene in the morning, assuming any of the resort is left standing around us."

His grin felt a little flat but it was genuine. That's why he'd handpicked Elena Moore—she had a pragmatism he appreciated. Especially when all he really wanted to do was text Cara and see if she'd still meet him for a drink in his room.

"That's a great idea." Without hesitation, he grabbed his phone and typed a message.

He hit Send, stood and gathered his laptop and other stuff, which had somehow become strewn across the table.

If Cara wasn't already asleep, he'd get a chance to blow off some of his personal frustration. The professional frustration would have to wait until dawn.

Like a teenager, he held his phone in his hand, screen up, so he'd see the return text from Cara the moment it arrived.

Nothing.

Maybe she was making a point, refusing to answer because it was way past nine o'clock and he'd made such a big deal about punctuality.

He dashed to his room without an umbrella. The wind nearly knocked him sideways, but he finally got a hand on the door and pushed his way inside, already soaking wet.

Cara would be soaking wet too by the time she got to his room—if he could entice her out of her snit.

That put the cap on it. She'd be wet, sexy and all the things he'd been fantasizing about since last night.

Once he got off the elevator and into his room, he texted her again.

Weary all of a sudden, he slumped on the love seat to

wait for Cara, too tired to pretend he wanted only the carnal pleasures to be had in her arms, when in truth, he'd be happy if she'd just be with him awhile. As a business owner, surely she'd understand his drive to be self-made—no family gravy train required—and would also be sympathetic to his failures. She didn't look to him for strategy, results, dollar signs, fill in the blank.

He needed her tonight—for more than sex.

How strange was *that*?

By ten forty-five that knock on the door hadn't come. She wasn't going to show, leaving him to decide whether he had the energy left to hunt her down.

Cara spun on her toe to pace in the other direction, phone clutched in her hand so tightly, the screen might be permanently damaged. The room was unfortunately too small to unload the high level of anxiety and frustration coursing through her blood.

"That carpet is going to start crying before too long," Meredith commented without looking up from her tablet, where she was watching *Bridget Jones* for the four hundredth time. "Why are you still here? Keith texted you like twenty minutes ago."

"I can't do it."

She couldn't physically move toward the door. Couldn't text him back. Couldn't make a decision to save her life. This was it, the line in the sand, and she had no idea what would happen if she stepped over it.

This bout of indecision had started the moment she left Keith earlier and then had grown to something monstrous as the day dragged on. Part of her had hoped Keith would be too busy to meet up so she could avoid the line as long as possible. Regardless, Meredith had bossed Cara into a slinky thong and matching bra, then forcibly shoved her arms into a low-cut sundress.

It was fine. Keith might not even call.

Then her phone had beeped and flipped her into panic mode instantly.

"Can't do what? Let a hot man make you feel amazing?" Meredith rolled her eyes. "You're certifiable."

She was. "I am not."

Anyone who would open themselves up to being crushed again, who'd decided she wanted to see what love felt like in a relationship where that wasn't on offer, could easily be labeled crazy. Anyone who would pass up the opportunity to be with a man who'd made it clear he wanted her, trusted her and of all things *cared* about her was crazy times two.

The problem was she didn't know which one this summons would lead to. And she couldn't say the same about her feelings toward Keith, not 100 percent. After all, she'd thought she loved him before, only to find out nothing was as she'd told herself. And she certainly didn't trust him. Which left two consenting adults having an island fling with no pressures and no promises.

Or did it?

Cara moaned and sank to the floor. "He told me he cares about me in the same breath as saying neither of us has the luxury of a relationship right now. What does that mean? Maybe he'd be open to it later? Or was it just to get me into bed?"

"Asking the wrong person."

"Well, I can't ask Keith. He's the one who got me all confused in the first place."

She would have sworn she had it all figured out before coming to Grace Bay. Cara Chandler-Harris Designs was a business she'd created to get over Keith. And as a result, she'd found something she loved. Something she was good at. Something that fulfilled her aching soul.

But she'd never expected it to take the place of a relationship. She'd never expected Keith to come back in her life and show her she didn't know diddly-squat about what was supposed to happen after the "I-dos."

She'd never expected to want to learn with Keith by her side.

Her sister snorted. "What in the world is there to be confused about?"

"What's going to happen next?" Keith wasn't marriage material. But then what if she wasn't either? "What if I sleep with him and we end up with completely different ideas about where our relationship is—"

"Oh, honey, you're going about this all wrong." Meredith ditched her tablet and put a hand to her chin as if about to impart sage advice. "Stop being such a girl. You are woman, hear you roar. Get that man naked and horizontal and use him all up. Then after he's rested, do it again. Do your gender proud and take what you want."

Cara's mouth twisted into a wry smile. "Is that the secret?"

"There's no secret. You're thinking about this too much. Don't let the past ruin what you can have now. And really don't let the future mess up the present. That hasn't even happened yet."

"Because you're such a relationship expert?" That wasn't fair and it had more to do with how closemouthed her sister always was about her own love life, or lack thereof. Meredith's interaction with men started and ended in the bedroom, but that didn't give Cara an excuse to be mean.

She started to apologize but her sister cut her off.

"No." A shadow passed over Meredith's face. "Because I'm an expert in messing them up. That's how I know what not to do."

According to Meredith, obsessing about the plan fell squarely in the category of What Not to Do. And maybe her sister was right. Cara bit her lip.

Cara's design business filled her with purpose and gave

her a level of satisfaction she'd never known. Maybe it wasn't such a bad thing to take that and run...straight to Keith. This was Grace Bay, not Houston, and Cara could do whatever she wanted. Be whomever she wanted. If Cara Chandler-Harris could start her own business, she could have an island fling with her ex, too.

No plan needed.

Then, when it was over, *she* could walk away. The possibility of making that choice was empowering. What did she have to lose, really?

Meredith jerked her head at the door. "Get going and pray he's not already passed out from boredom."

Cara took a deep breath. She *could* do this. Or at least she could knock on Keith's door. One step at a time.

Tap, tap, tap.

Keith woke instantly from his uncomfortable catnap on the love seat, heart tripping. The light knock that had roused him could be only one person—Cara.

He yanked open the door and eyed the fully dressed woman on the other side. "You're late. That means you lose an article of clothing for every minute."

His already-surging blood pumped faster as he surveyed her. She was indeed wet. But not wet enough.

"I seem to recall you said you'd come looking for me," she said primly and stood her umbrella against the outside wall. "Which you did not."

"Now who's being logical?" He held out his hand and when she took it, he pulled her inside the room, where he'd lowered the lights. Soft jazz music, which he'd switched on earlier before he fell asleep, played in the background. If she'd warned him of her imminent arrival, he could have done a little more to set the mood.

Of course, it would help if she'd tell him what sort of mood to set. A woman's extreme tardiness usually didn't bode well when a drink invitation clearly came with benefits.

"Nice," she commented as she followed him into the room. "Being the boss has its privileges."

Small talk didn't scream "I'm into you" either.

She sank gracefully into a leather chair near the lounge table, pointedly ignoring the love seat, where they could have both easily fit. And could have indulged in a little foreplay.

Which might have been the point. But if she wasn't here to pick up where they'd left off earlier this morning, why *was* she here?

"I didn't think you were coming."

Now, why had he opened that can of worms? Obviously, if she'd dropped him butt-first on a Tilt-a-Whirl she couldn't have thrown him more off balance than she had with her late arrival.

Cara cleared her throat. "I didn't think I was coming either. But I'm here now."

Despite the ambiguity, he could roll with that. Something loosened in his chest. She *was* here and that was enough. If it led to more, great. If not, that was okay, too.

For the first time in their relationship, he genuinely wanted to spend time with her, talk to her, hear her opinions and—

God, what was *wrong* with him?

He poured her a glass of wine from the same label she'd enjoyed last night and handed it to her, then took the other chair, suddenly feeling oddly as if they were on a first date.

And maybe they kind of were. At least it was a first date between Keith and this new woman Cara had become. A first date after wiping the slate clean of all their disastrous history, including Keith's mistakes. Perhaps she'd come to that conclusion as well—hence the distance.

She'd earned the right to be romanced, no matter how many times they'd seen each other naked in the past.

"I'm curious about something." He sipped wine to set the conversational mood, which would serve to put her at ease. "What do you hope to get from this expo? Professionally?"

Surprise flew into her expression. "Exposure, of course."

He grinned in spite of the strange tension between them. "I realize that. I mean, what are your goals? Fifteen percent increase in orders? By when? What's the measure of your cost investment versus payoff? That sort of thing."

"Why do you want to know?"

Her tone sounded the opposite of someone letting their guard down.

"Because I'm interested in you," he blurted out. Too touchy-feely and now he felt as if he'd stepped in quicksand. *Backpedal.* "And on the off chance the expo is canceled, I'd like to know what your losses will be."

Better. Keep it about work. That he understood.

"I don't need you to cover them, if that's where you're headed."

"No, that wasn't my intent at all." He downed half his wine in hopes it would get his brain and tongue in sync or at least dull his wits enough to not care how badly he was botching this.

Maybe he should shut up and kiss her. They'd never had problems communicating *that* way. But the vibe was so weird, he hesitated. Besides, he'd told her to stop assuming all he cared about was sex—and somehow they were at a place where that remained true, so he should practice what he preached.

After a deep breath, he tried again. "Businesses intrigue me. The flow of capital, margins, profit-loss statements. Spreadsheets are my crack. It's why I like consulting, because I can dig into what makes a company live and breathe from a ten-thousand-foot view. When we dated before, our common interests were always other things. Now we have something new in common. I want to talk to you about it."

The tension melted from her face. "Keith, that's the sweetest thing you've ever said to me."

"Uh…what?" He watched her as she set her glass down on the table, gaze squarely on him. And it was noticeably warmer. Then she rose and skirted the table to lean over and kiss him soundly on the lips.

He was too busy trying to not stare down her still-damp dress to kiss her back, but then she touched his cheek in a brief caress and thoroughly ensnared him with the expression on her face. He couldn't look away.

"You basically said that you see me as an equal. That's the best compliment you could have given me. Thank you." She settled into the love seat instead of returning to her chair and swirled her fingertips across the next cushion in blatant invitation.

That was some magic wine he'd selected. He switched seats gladly, still clueless how his neurotic love of entrepreneurship had somehow shifted the mood.

"The truth is," she drawled, "I don't have good projections for this expo. I have enough of a marketing background to know that exposure is king, but difficult to quantify. I'd love to have some solid numbers, but it's hard to be the CEO, CFO, chief marketing officer and actually get around to designing dresses at the same time."

"I'll help you," he offered instantly, surreptitiously inhaling her exotic perfume. "It'll be fun. Really."

Exotic with enough of Cara laced through it to thoroughly intoxicate him. He couldn't remember a blessed thing about what kind of perfume she'd worn before. Because he'd never noticed it. Not like this, as if it was part of the full, potent package of the woman.

She rolled her eyes without malice. "Only you would call

that fun. It's an interesting proposition. I'd kill for your expertise, but in lieu of that, I'd pay for it. Name your price."

"No strings attached." And he meant it. "I insist. It'll be a thank-you for helping me out earlier."

It was the least he could do, and it made him pathetically grateful to have a concrete way to repay her for organizing the mock wedding. And for helping with the room inventory. And for her freely given forgiveness, which he hadn't realized would come to mean so much.

"Wow. If I'd have known that would be the reward, I'd have volunteered to clean the oven with my tongue." She slid a glance down his torso. "But I can't let you do it for free. I insist on tit for tat. If you won't take money, what other form of barter could we possibly cook up?"

Instantly, the strange first-date, why-was-she-here vibe vanished and everything fell into place.

"I'm sure we could come up with something," he murmured and reached up to finger a lock of her curling, damp hair. "But I owe you. Not the other way around. After all, you're the one who had to dash through the rain to get here."

"No problem." She smiled. "It was worth it."

"Yeah?" The thought warmed him enormously.

Placing a delicate palm against his thigh, she leaned in, peering up through lowered lashes. "Totally. You have air-conditioning."

He bit back a snort. "Yes, among other luxuries. Let me show you."

Before she could open her smart mouth again, he tipped her chin up and laid his lips on hers. Her soft sigh bled through him, energizing him.

The long, stressful day melted away as he fell into her. Her soft lips firmed and she came alive, hands in his hair, body snugged against his. Hot spikes of desire exploded in his groin and he groaned.

It had been a while. Even longer since he'd had a woman

in his arms who intrigued him as much as this one. Their bodies knew each other intimately, but the nuances of this new Cara bled into the experience, heightening it. Heating it. What other new things would he uncover?

She pulled his shirt from his pants and her fingertips slid along his sensitized back, dipping lower. His lungs contracted and his brain went fuzzy.

"Wait." He drew back but Cara's kiss-stung lips and mussed hair called to him. He resisted diving back in. Barely.

I want to love you like you deserve. Like I should have the first time.

He dropped to his knees between her legs and eagerly she scooted forward, aiming for his mouth, as if to kiss him again. Oh no, not this time. He held up a palm to stop her and gently leaned her back, ensuring she rested comfortably against the couch cushions. He kissed her throat, working his way down until he hit fabric.

"Let me," he murmured and drew down the shoulder straps of her sleeveless dress and bra, baring her breasts.

Gorgeous. Her nipples peaked under his gaze and he swallowed back the urge to spout poetry. As if he even knew any, especially a verse good enough to describe how magnificent the sight of half-dressed Cara was.

"I could look at you for hours." But he wanted to touch, so he traced the lines of her uncovered torso a bit more reverently than he'd intended, but oh well. As he enjoyed himself, he worshipped her with his gaze.

She watched him, a hint of curiosity in her expression. As if she couldn't quite figure out what he meant to accomplish, which unsettled him. Had he never made it all about her in the past? Their physical relationship had been satisfying for them both. Hadn't it?

It didn't matter. She'd come to him tonight and regardless of her motivation, he was going to make it cataclysmic for her. Mitchell the Missile would hit this target or die trying.

Eight

Rain beat against the window, melding with the jazz music to create a rhythmic, sensual tempo that seemed to infuse Cara's blood. Or maybe that was the heat in Keith's expression as he swept her with another gaze full of promise and wicked intent.

When she'd knocked on the door, she'd expected to have a nice evening with Keith that included a satisfying round of intimacy. In the past, he'd proved to be an energetic, generous bed partner. They got naked, it was hot, they both climaxed and that was it—why should it be any different this time? One island fling coming up.

And then he'd changed it all up by starting this couch seduction. Keith didn't do slow, or at least he never had before. And that's when she got the first inkling this evening wasn't going to be anything like she'd expected.

Without warning, Keith lowered his head to her breast and swirled his tongue across her flesh, then latched on to suck with quick little pulls. Breath whooshed from her lungs, her back arching involuntarily to meet his lips. Her nipple drove deeper in his mouth, his teeth scraping at her sensitized breast, and she moaned.

Thick, dense heat gathered at her core and spun outward, enflaming her skin.

He switched to her other nipple, laving it sensuously as if he had all the time in the world, while she fought to keep from sliding to the floor in a puddle of sensation. His palms gripped her rib cage, jutting her breasts forward. He licked and sucked, alternating as he pleased, while she squirmed, head lolling back against the cushions until she could hardly breathe, hardly think.

Moans spurted from her lips, and nonsensical phrases floated through her mind. Shouldn't she be reaching for him, to pleasure him in kind?

Her leaden arms refused to move and sensation swamped her. She had no idea her breasts were such an erogenous zone, but then no man had ever expended so much effort demonstrating it to her.

As often as Keith commented how much she'd changed in two years, he'd seemed pretty much like the same guy. Until tonight.

He raised his head, gaze hot with unfulfilled longing and mysterious intent. With a gentle lift of her bottom, he pulled off her dress in an impressive one-handed move and threw it over his shoulder. Rocking forward on his knees, he bent and aimed for the juncture of her thighs.

What was he doing? He couldn't…he'd always respected her discom—

White-hot sparks exploded at her core as he put his mouth over her center, nibbling her through her panties.

She almost bucked off the cushion. Firm hands to her hips held her in place against the couch as he tongued her. He had to stop. This wasn't…she couldn't…and then the exquisite torture ratcheted up a notch as his strong fingertips slid beneath the string of her thong to grip her rear and shove her more firmly against his mouth. His tongue tunneled under the fabric to find her bare flesh, and his light touch teased her in a place no man's fingers had ever teased.

It was too much. And oh so amazing.

Hands in his hair, she held on as he flung her into the heavens. Again and again, he drove his tongue against her nub, then deep in her core, and back to where he started. Bright pinpoints of light blurred her vision, and the cresting wave broke over her in a thick flood of release.

Panting, she scrabbled for purchase against Keith's shoulders, desperate to hold on to *something*. As her body cooled and her heart rate slowed, her mind decided to start functioning again.

And it was turning over the fact that while it had always been good with Keith, it hadn't been like *that*.

When she could speak, she eyed him. "What was that all about?"

His eyebrows shot up and his satisfied smile widened. "Well, I hoped it would be fairly obvious. Do you need a repeat, so you can figure it out? Because I'd be happy to help."

Her lips involuntarily curved up in response. "You know what I mean. That was not standard operating procedure between us."

He shrugged and picked up one of her feet to unbuckle her stiletto, still grinning as if he had plenty more where that came from. "We had busy lives in Houston. We didn't live together. It was hard to justify taking my time when I always had a twelve- or fourteen-hour day ahead of me."

The shoe slid from her foot and he started rubbing the arch, which felt so amazing, she groaned. "Because tomorrow isn't going to be a backbreaker of a day?"

"No. Hear that?" He tilted his head to the window, where rain lashed at the pane and wind whined through palm trees. "That's the sound of a storm giving me all the time in the world to do exactly as I please. I've got all night and a strong interest in getting...creative with how I spend it."

Her tummy began humming. Her mama had raised her right and there were some things a lady didn't do. Intimacy was something to cherish, something to create with the right person, and she'd never slept with a man she couldn't imagine being with forever.

But this wasn't her mama's island fling. It wasn't as if Cara had a true aversion to being adventurous—she'd just never had the right opportunity. There were limits to what you could realistically do and then look someone in the face every morning for the rest of your life.

But tonight wasn't about the rest of her life. And she was safe with Keith. What better opportunity was there to take what she wanted and use him all up, as Meredith would say.

It would make it that much easier to walk away afterward.

With renewed interest, she cocked her head. "That sounds promising. Tell me more."

His wicked grin curled her toes as he swept her with a pointed once-over. "Remember your answer to the newlywed game about your favorite position?"

"Missionary works," she shot back. "What's wrong with that?"

"Nothing." He kissed her foot and moved to her ankle with little butterfly caresses of his lips that teased and excited at the same time. "But there are so many more we can try."

The idea took root and blossomed. But there was one small factor she couldn't figure out. "Why now? What's the occasion?"

They'd certainly never had such a conversation before.

Her other shoe hit the floor and Keith draped one leg over his shoulder, then bent the other one toward her torso, opening her up to his hot perusal. She let him roll with it and got a delicious little thrill for her effort.

"You're a businesswoman now. Independent. I cannot stress enough what a huge turn-on that is."

Oh my. So designing a few wedding gowns had suddenly cast her into a whole new level of hotness?

The thought was fascinating. He wasn't turned on by her sexy lingerie—he'd barely noticed it. No shade of lipstick or hair color could have given her the slightest edge. Instead, something intangible beneath her skin had brought about this new realm of possibility. The best part? It would never fade because it was internal.

The fact that he found her sexier because of her accomplishments was turning her on, too, picking up the remnants of her earlier orgasm and fanning the flames. There was entirely too much talking going on, and it was totally her fault. But choosing to be adventurous and doing it were two different things.

Before she could decide what to do first, he turned his unshaven jaw into her thigh and abraded her skin lightly, then sucked. It was slightly painful but thoroughly thrilling, and the answering tugs at her core shocked her at their intensity.

As he edged closer to her panties, he left a trail of light marks in his wake. When his lips hit the fabric, he glanced up through his lashes. "I've always wanted to do that."

"Is that how this works?" she asked, her voice catching over the tangle of stimulation in her throat. "We just do whatever we want?"

"Yes." He nodded succinctly. "Take charge of your pleasure, Cara. I insist. Be in control. I will not complain."

Emboldened by his frank instructions, she rolled her hips, brushing her panties against his jaw. "Do that again, but without the thong."

His gaze heated. "Liked that, did you?"

Without another word, he hooked the strings of her panties and yanked them off, resettling between her thighs, but unlike the first time, gentleness didn't seem to be a part of the agenda.

He gripped her hips, pulled her to the edge of the couch and pushed her thighs apart. His tongue raked her still-sensitive nub and she gasped, bowing up. Then he slid two fingers into her and twisted. The eruption of heat nearly made her black out.

She swallowed a very unladylike curse, hips swiveling with a mind of their own as he shoved her to the edge of desire. And beyond. The release rocketed through her, encompassing her whole body.

With the aftershocks still gripping her, Keith murmured, "You know what's really good? Me inside you before you've fully come down."

This could be *better*? Half-blind, she sat up—how, she didn't know when all her bones had disappeared—and clawed at Keith's shirt, popping buttons as she stripped him out of it.

He pulled his arms from the fabric, and the motion propelled her off the love seat and into his lap. She took it as a sign to lock lips and lost herself in the dark, sizzling splendor of his kiss.

His strong, amazing lips. The things they'd done to her. The things they were *still* doing. He tasted of wine and earthiness, and it was exquisite.

She pulled off his pants, and in her urgency got the legs all tangled up. He was no help, grappling with one side while she yanked on the other. Finally, her questing hands found bare flesh and she stroked every inch she touched.

Keith's head tipped back and he groaned. Her lips curved up, surprising her. It was heady to cause a man so controlled and so big and so masculine to feel pleasure.

"Now," she said and pushed him back against the carpet, then mounted him.

Wordlessly, he held up two fingers with a foil packet caught between them. Yes, of course he'd be on top of that. She shoved aside the reminder that they of all people shouldn't take any chances and paused as he put on the condom.

Thighs wide, she guided his body until everything clicked and he filled her instantly. Oh, yes, that *was* good. Still sensitized, still damp, the additional friction and pressure nearly set her off again.

Throwing her own head back in ecstasy, she found a rhythm that got a guttural sound of approval from Keith. Wantonly, she glanced down at him spread out underneath her like an offering to a goddess, and the power of it shot through her.

He reached up to touch her and she shook her head, lacing her fingers with his to pin them to the carpet. Despite knowing that he could break free any moment, she reveled in the ability to command a 190-pound man covered in sinewy muscles.

His eyes shut in apparent pleasure as she changed the angle again, driving her hips harder, and all of it coalesced into a bright, hot ball at their joined bodies. Nonsense words flowed from her throat as the orgasm built and exploded in an epicenter of ripples.

Totally sapped, she collapsed on Keith's chest as he cried out with his own release. His arms came around her, binding her tightly to him as he spent himself.

Chests heaving together, they lay torso to torso. She couldn't have moved if the hotel room caught fire.

"That," Keith huffed, "was un-freaking-believable."

It had been. Keith never talked like that, but she agreed—no other term could describe it.

"And then some."

But only because Keith had encouraged her to spread her wings. Only because he'd told her how hot it was. Only because this was a fling and nothing more.

The thought made her a little sad all at once. Why couldn't sex between them be adventurous and fulfilling and wonderful while they were a couple?

Well, because it didn't work that way, obviously. Either it could be tender and meaningful or it could be a smoking-hot fling. And honestly, it hadn't been all that tender the first time around, when she'd thought they were in love.

"As much as I enjoyed the floor, I'm a little carpet burned," Keith murmured and stroked her hair. "Shall we move to the bed?"

Cheek to his pectoral muscle, she listened to his heart rate slow. Did that mean he was good and rested already? "I've got another round in me."

He groaned and it was not one of anticipation. "Dawn is going to come much sooner than I'd like and I'm afraid storm cleanup is going to be brutal. What if we just go to sleep?"

Sleep? Here? That was the opposite of a good idea. As if doused by a bucket of cold water, sense returned to her brain. Rolling off Keith carefully, she scouted around for her dress, found it and yanked it over her head without taking the extra time to don her bra and panties.

"I, ah…think I'll head back to my room."

Still naked and apparently not interested in fixing that, Keith sat up, muscles bunching and flexing. Dang it if he wasn't the sexiest male on the planet, with or without clothes. Why was she leaving again?

"Your room doesn't have an air conditioner," he reminded her. "Stay. I'd like to see your face in the morning."

Oh yeah. *That* was why. "No, it's better we keep this expectation free. Sleepovers are like the gateway. It starts feeling like we're a couple again and neither of us has the *luxury* of that."

Wincing at her catty tone, she gathered all her things and headed for the door before he could say anything. "Thanks, Mitchell. That was amazing. See you tomorrow."

The storm nearly blew her sideways, dousing her instantly. As she dashed through the rain to the other tower—because in her panic she'd fled without her umbrella—she had to admit that part of her wished they did have the luxury of more and it was something they both wanted.

They'd tried a just-starting-to-date relationship. They'd tried being an engaged couple. They'd tried hot, no holds barred and no strings.

And against all good reason, she wanted to know what it would be like with Keith if they were in love. If birth control wasn't so critical… But it *was* critical, because she couldn't trust him with anything other than her body. It didn't matter if he cared about her or had other interests besides sex, because she couldn't let him hurt her again.

She sighed as she mounted the stairs to her room, dripping water and despondency all over the place. Maybe no strings got easier. She'd have to try harder to not care that Keith's expression had resembled granite when he'd watched her leave.

Cara Chandler-Harris Designs would never walk out on her, never disappoint her. What did she need with a man long-term anyway?

Keith let Cara go and spent the night watching the weather radar on an endless loop. It mirrored the chaos in his head perfectly.

Too restless to sleep, he prowled around the suite looking for something to punch, because he feared that was the only way he'd expel the black mood he'd fallen into when Cara had waltzed out the door.

It was for the best. She was absolutely right. They weren't in a relationship. Sleepovers weren't a good idea. When the storm passed, Keith would be overloaded with revised expo plans and Cara would be in the way. She knew that, had made herself scarce, and he should completely respect and appreciate it.

But all he could think about was how he'd yearned to slide into sleep with her sated body nestled against his, breathing in sync.

Disgusted and furious for no reason, he took a long shower and forced himself to crawl into bed, where he listened to the wind howl and caught snatches of shut-eye, only to bolt awake because he'd dreamed Cara had come back, blubbering apologies and begging him to let her stay. But it was only the crack of branches outside or the tap of rain against the window that, in his delirium, he'd mistaken for her.

Dawn brought with it an even blacker mood.

Overnight, the storm whirled out into the interior of the Caribbean to wreak havoc with Cuba and Grand Cayman. The resort hadn't lost power, which Regent executives would be quite pleased to note since Keith had insisted on installing top-of-the-line generators and storm-proof wiring.

But the pool resembled tree limb soup with a generous garnish of dirt and leaves. The permanent wedding gazebo was gone—the storm had even ripped away the concrete moorings, then filled the holes with sand. A new one would have to be ordered and reanchored, but obviously better and differently.

The door to the sports equipment shed hung drunkenly from one hinge and the floor sat underneath two inches of water. Fortunately, the kayaks, surfboards and other gear seemed no worse for wear. They were supposed to get wet, after all.

The outdoor bar was weatherproof, or it was supposed to be. Scrapes marred the surface as if the wind had dragged tree limbs across it. The bar would have to be refinished, and the list went on and on. Alice scurried after him as he barked out orders and observations. Eventually, they organized resources and the challenges began to look a little more doable.

Sometime around midmorning, Keith holed up in his office to respond to email. Coffee and a solid plan had improved his mood. When Cara knocked on the open door, he even managed a smile.

"Got a minute?" she asked and leaned on the doorjamb.

He nodded and let the image of Cara's naked body astride his flash through his mind because he wanted to and because it was still powerful. What had started out as a method to make sure she had an amazing experience had somehow morphed into the best sex of his life.

"What's up?" He cleared his throat, though it was pretty useless since the huskiness in his voice was due to the raging erection he'd just given himself with a simple memory.

"I was curious about the expo. What are the plans?"

Dry Cara wasn't any less sexy and alluring than a wet Cara. She appeared well rested, as if sleep had come easily to her, and today's dress hugged the curves he'd eagerly reacquainted himself with last night.

"The airport is scheduled to reopen tomorrow morning. So we'll go on, albeit late." He sat back in his chair and wished they could have had this conversation over breakfast. Because she'd stayed with him overnight. Pathetic. Why was he torturing himself with fanciful scenarios? "I'm sending out the revised schedule to all the expo guests and vendors now. You're on the email distribution list."

"The resort doesn't seem too worse for wear. Have you got a good handle on the cleanup?"

He shrugged. "Elena's got it. She's corralling the

groundskeepers as we speak and we'll have to adjust a few of the events. But we've got a promising start."

"That's good to hear." Cara flowed across the threshold and shut the door behind her with a wicked gleam in her eye. "Hope you'll pardon the interruption then."

Before he could get a word in edgewise, she rounded the desk and climbed into his lap.

Hungrily, she fused her lips to his and kissed him open-mouthed, tongue sliding against his. Rough and wild, she savored him and he groaned under her commanding offensive.

His body instantly responded, spreading heat and fire outward from his already primed erection to encompass every organ. Her fingers worked his buttons clumsily until she apparently gave up and ripped the fabric wide to slide her hands along his torso, around the sides and up his back. Everything she touched leaped under her palms, crackling with energy.

Then she dipped into his pants to curve his shaft into her fisted hand. He pulsed and nearly lost complete control.

"Wait," he bit out. "I…wasn't expecting you and—"

"It's okay." She pulled a wrapped condom from inside her bra. "A gift from Meredith."

Breath he hadn't realized he'd been holding whooshed out. Thankfully, Cara got the necessity of being careful. No ties this time. "I really, really like your sister."

Cara grinned. "I'll tell her you said so. Later. I want you to take me right here on your desk. Now," she commanded.

Sweeter words had never been spoken. Quickly, he stood with Cara in his arms and situated her on the desk, thighs spread wide. He stepped between them and yanked her dress and bra down in one motion. Her gorgeous breasts spilled free and he shoved one between his teeth.

She thrust against his mouth, moaning, and he shut his eyes at the perfection of her taste.

"I want you naked," she rasped, and her lithe fingers undid his pants, dropping them to the floor. Her hand closed around him for the second time but nothing hindered her movement, and his breath hitched as she stroked him.

This hot little morning quickie was about to be very over if she kept doing that.

To distract her, he stripped off her dress and threw it… somewhere and then she was spread out on his desk wearing nothing at all, so achingly beautiful it hurt his chest to look at her.

I need you. Right now. Later. Tomorrow. Maybe longer than that.

His fingers shook as he rolled on the condom. From need. From emotions he couldn't name. From the sheer desire this woman evoked. He bent one of her legs to open her farther but she smiled wickedly and shook her head.

"Not like this." She flipped over on her stomach, arching her back and glancing over her shoulder at him like a naughty fantasy come to life. "Like this."

Legs spread wide in invitation, she jiggled her rear. His eyelids slammed closed involuntarily and he forced them open because no way was he missing a moment of this visual delight.

"Keith, hurry. Take me now and make me come like you did last night."

Groaning, he slid into her slowly, relishing the tight heat. But she was having none of that. Impatiently, she rolled her hips, drawing him deeper, and her little cries inflamed him with urgency.

Gripping her hips, he filled her again and again until she went rigid and then convulsed around him, squeezing a shattering climax from the depths of his soul.

His midsection contracted as he emptied himself, leaving nothing behind. Almost unable to stand, he braced his arms against the desk, one on each side of the amazing woman before him. Cheek to the blotter, she closed her eyes and let a blissful, smug smile bloom.

She was thoroughly enjoying the liberties he'd insisted she take. Good. He was, too.

It hit him like a two-by-four to the head—their affair wasn't so great this time around just because she was so hot and ready and taking charge, but because they were coming together as equals. He'd never had that before.

When he thought he could move without collapsing to the floor in a jellified heap, he bent forward and laid his lips against her temple in a long kiss. "Maybe next time we'll make it to the bed."

I want you close to me while you dream.

"Been there, done that. No thanks. Next on my list is the hot tub out on your balcony."

Disappointment flared but he shoved it back. He was getting exactly what he'd asked for—what was there to be disappointed about?

"Done. Come by tonight." The last thing he needed was to spend another sleepless night after Cara left, but he was apparently incapable of saying no.

He helped Cara get dressed and drew on his ruined shirt. She pecked him on the cheek in what he assumed was good-bye and then dived in for a long, lingering kiss full of sensual promise that he couldn't have stepped away from if a category five hurricane hit.

Who could blame him for spitting out yes after yes? This new Cara blew his mind, in so many ways. And the more he tried to convince himself it was strictly sexual, the less he believed it.

This was a dangerous game to be playing in the midst of the rescheduled expo. Perhaps he should focus on that and not on this impossible dynamic between them. But as Cara's sexy backside disappeared through the door and

Keith contemplated how he'd get past Alice with the buttons hanging by threads from his shirt, he had a pretty good idea a hot tub was in his future.

Nine

The promised email was indeed in Cara's inbox when she returned to her room from Keith's office, not at all ashamed to have just experienced an amazing orgasm on the boss's desk with his staff milling around outside the door.

Cornering him in his lair had been the most daring thing she'd ever done. But she knew he wouldn't have shoved her out the door. It was part of what made this fling so great—she didn't have to wonder where she stood with Keith. Didn't have to worry he'd leave her again because she planned to ensure this relationship stayed fun and non-permanent, as he'd specified.

It was perfect.

And he'd never find out she'd cried herself to sleep last night, longing for it not to feel as if she'd sold her soul to the devil for a company with her name on it and an earth-shattering carnal affair with someone she'd probably never see again after the expo finished.

The expo's new schedule called for the bridal fashion

show on the second day, which was perfect. She and Meredith would be able to make the final alterations today and tomorrow, no problem...assuming Cara stayed out of Keith's office, that was.

Humming to cover a tightness in her throat she couldn't explain, Cara gathered the models and Meredith to go over the revised schedule for the next couple of days. She answered the understandable questions from the girls about accommodations and rescheduled return flights—Regent was footing the bill for any and all additional fees, a classy move that as a business owner without an unlimited expense fund, Cara appreciated.

Since she did have a business to run and her return to the States had been delayed, Cara sent the models off to relax and assigned Meredith the task of assessing the beach pavilion. If it had been damaged, they'd need a venue change or, barring that, an understanding of what might need to be adjusted in the fashion show itself.

Then she spent a much-needed hour going through some accounting paperwork and paying a few bills. While she was online, an email popped into her inbox containing messages sent to her via the contact form on her website.

Two requests for more information. Cara picked up her cell phone immediately and dialed the first potential customer. The bride-to-be answered, a rarity as she usually had to play phone tag for a few days. Cara spent several minutes chatting with the woman about her upcoming wedding, hoping to put Yvette, the prospective customer, at ease.

This was one of her favorite parts of being a dress designer. The brides were always so eager to talk to *anyone* about what was sure to be the best day of their lives and Cara loved to hear every last detail, especially because she got a good, clear sense of what kind of person the woman was. It helped her visualize the perfect dress. Plus, Cara loved weddings period.

"The theme of your wedding sounds almost ethereal," Cara commented after several minutes of prodding Yvette about the minutest details, even down to the favors. "I see you as the star of your own fairy tale, with a long train, lace bodice and sweetheart neckline. Stark white because you'll want to stand out against the off-white lilies."

Yvette sighed happily. "That sounds lovely. I knew you were the right one to create my dress when I saw that all your designs had princess names."

Cara smiled at Yvette's enthusiasm. "Was there a particular dress you liked in the online portfolio?"

Despite having nailed the high-level specifics a moment ago, much more went into the design than the train and color. They'd work through the details for several weeks before Cara picked up her shears.

"All of them. But I want something no one else has. A one-of-a-kind exclusive."

"Absolutely. That's no problem." Exclusive dresses took longer because Cara didn't have a set pattern, but any bride who asked for one never minded the wait. Or the cost.

True love paid the bills, but brides who wanted to keep up with other Houston brides put Cara in the black very early on.

Cara asked a few more follow-up questions and verified Yvette's email address in order to send design mockups once Cara created them. She ended the call and realized she hadn't once thought about her own halted wedding, nor felt the accompanying tug of sadness.

That was a vast improvement over the majority of the other calls she'd conducted in the course of the past eighteen months. It was a small triumph and she reveled in it for a moment.

She'd moved past it, once and for all. This business was hers and no one could take it away. Oddly, Keith had helped her begin viewing herself as a businesswoman, independent and in charge of her destiny. If she hadn't splashed head-first into this fling with him, no plan, no pressure, would she have gotten to this place?

It was a very interesting thought. Apparently Meredith was far smarter about matters of the heart than Cara had credited.

The second request for information listed a man's name as the contact—Nick Anderson. Interesting. Cara dialed the referenced phone number, wondering if she'd be discussing a bride's dress with the groom instead. There was always the unlikely possibility of one of her dresses ending up in a drag-queen revue. Either would be okay as long as the check cleared and her name was spelled right on any recommendations.

The call connected. "Ever After. Nick Anderson speaking."

Cara's tongue went numb. Ever After? As in the boutique retail outlet specializing in high-end wedding dresses— *that* Ever After?

"Um." Cara cleared her throat. "This is Cara Chandler-Harris. I'm a wedding dress designer. You requested that I contact you through my website."

"Yes, I did." His voice warmed. "That was fast. I only did so a couple of hours ago. I'm unexpectedly planning to be at the Regent Resorts Bridal Expo in Grace Bay to-morrow and hoped to meet with you. Are you still partici-pating?"

"I… Yes, of course. I'm already here actually."

"Great. The storm delay caused a shuffle on our end, which is why I'm now attending, so I thought I'd verify."

"Right." Cara had been reduced to monosyllables. Not an auspicious start to…whatever this was. "What is the purpose of the meeting, if I may ask?"

"Well, it's a little preliminary, but our focus at Ever After is changing. We'd like to discuss the possibility of featuring your dresses in our stores. I saw your name on the vendor list for the Expo and since I'd never heard of you, I looked up your work. I'm very impressed."

The phone slipped from Cara's hand and she scrambled to pick it up. "Thank you," she squawked, her heart galloping a mile a minute.

Tropical storm Mark's trajectory over the island had proved to be a blessing in disguise.

"Seems like fate that we'll be in the same place this week. I hope you'll be able to give me a few minutes of your time."

"I wouldn't miss it."

Cara ended the call and sat there, dazed, for a moment. Then she leaped to her feet.

Keith. She had to tell him.

She couldn't wait to see that killer smile bloom when she announced the news. Oh, sure, the deal with Ever After could fall through, but still. Someone with real clout in the wedding industry praised her designs and wanted to meet with her. As a potential business partner.

The meeting alone made Cara Chandler-Harris Designs real in a way that she hadn't experienced yet. Up until now, it had almost felt like a hobby that happened to net her some cash and afforded her a fun way to do it. But Ever After Boutiques was the big time, exactly the kind of attention she'd hoped to attract by participating in the expo.

Keith would congratulate her and say he was proud. Then he'd tell her it was sexy that she'd made a career out of her design business.

Laughing like a loon, she dashed through the pool area, nearly running smack into Meredith.

"Whoa." Her sister put up her hands, tottering back on her stilettos until she regained her balance. "Where's the fire?"

"Oh, I have the best news." Breathless, she started to

skirt Meredith, hoping Keith was still in his office. Okay, that was probably not a very good locale for a conversation, actually…

"Well?" With a cheeky grin, Meredith jammed a hand on her hip. And waited.

Eyes wide, Cara stared at her. "Well, what?"

"Don't make me beg. What is it?"

It finally dawned on her. Meredith thought Cara had been looking for *her* to share the news. "Oh. I was actually on my way—"

She swallowed the rest before she admitted out loud that she'd wanted to share this triumph with Keith first. Before her sister, who was also her best friend. And her assistant. "Never mind."

"Never mind you're not going to tell me? That's not fair. You got me all excited for nothing."

Cara rolled her eyes. "It's not that big of a deal," she lied. The last thing she wanted was to hurt her sister's feelings. "I just got word of a potential proposition for my dresses that I need to discuss with Keith. Because he offered to advise me on my business plan."

That last part may have come out a little too rushed, but it *was* true. And it was better than admitting she'd never even once thought of telling Meredith.

"Uh-huh." A knowing light glinted in Meredith's gaze. "You've got it bad, sister."

The joy of having someone who could read her so well. Cara sighed. "I do not."

That was such a lie she couldn't even keep a straight face as she delivered it.

As wake-up calls went, it was not pleasant. When exactly had she fallen off the sex-and-nothing-else wagon?

Well, she should climb back on, stat.

Hooking arms with Meredith, she reversed course and returned with her sister to their room, chatting up the call with Nick Anderson. Keith would never find out she'd accidentally started thinking of him as someone to share things with.

She deliberately stayed away from Keith the rest of the day. Fortuitous, since she made significant progress on the critical tasks for the fashion show in two days. She also got a lot of practice at squelching the ache inside that she feared meant she missed Keith.

At nine o'clock, the expected text message from the man in question arrived, inviting her to his room. Period. No further explanation, as if he knew she'd come running when he called.

Yeah, so he was correct and sticking her tongue out at the phone didn't make the fact that she'd been sitting here yearning to see him any less true.

Cara borrowed Meredith's bikini, which roughly resembled three postage stamps attached with string, figuring she wouldn't have it on longer than about five minutes, and belted a trench coat over it.

Keith tossed his head back against the fiberglass edge of the hot tub, eyes closed as he struggled to drag oxygen into his starved lungs. Cara splashed to her own recovery spot a few feet away, likely as depleted as he was.

The value of high-powered water jets and a daring spirit could not be exaggerated.

"You're amazing," he murmured without opening his eyes. "I didn't really think you'd go for that last suggestion."

"That'll teach you to bluff," she said, her voice low and seductive with a ragged edge that spoke to how vigorously she'd proved that particular point.

"I wasn't bluffing. Just really, really hopeful." And he'd been really, really rewarded.

More splashing alerted him that Cara was on the move.

He forced an eye open to glimpse her climbing out of the hot tub. "Where are you going? We just got started."

Why was she always so eager to disappear? Was his company that objectionable when he wasn't naked?

She chuckled. "I think twice was enough for tonight. Busy day tomorrow."

"Wait." He captured her hand before she could take another step and lost his train of thought for a moment. Water rolled from her bare body, running from her hair in long trails down her torso. One drop hung from a pert nipple, begging for his tongue, and he hardened all over again.

Simply looking at her hurt, way down on the inside where it couldn't be salved.

He should let her leave. The expo would begin in the morning and Regent executives would be on the property before nine. Everything had to go off without a hitch, and his attention to the minutest detail couldn't be more critical.

"Stay and have a drink instead. One glass of wine. You'll sleep better, I promise."

Don't leave. Not this time. If he could only put his finger on why it mattered so much to him, *he'd* sure sleep a lot better.

"That's not what we're doing here. Right?" A line appeared between her eyebrows as she pulled her hand from his. "That's what you said. No pressure, no relationship."

"Oh, come on." He flashed a quick grin, though it was a little forced. Somehow her constant and immediate exits seemed to be driven from a mixed-up view of his expectations. "No pressure isn't the same as no conversation. We can hang out and talk. That's part of what's making sex so great between us, don't you think? All the nonnaked time we've had thus far?"

In what world did it make sense that he was arguing with her about staying for a *drink* instead of trying to sweet-talk her clothes off? But here they were, in the alternate universe of Grace Bay, where Cara eagerly bared her body—which he fully appreciated—but balked at anything else.

"I do like your wine." Indecision rippled across her expression. "One drink?"

"Or two. Who's counting?"

"I don't have any clothes."

As if that was a good argument against it. But his still-scrambled brain couldn't latch on to a good enough argument for it.

Stay. Because you want to. Because you want more.

But what if he reached out and she slammed him down? Or worse, thought "more" was code for a white picket fence and another diamond ring?

A drink was all he could reasonably offer until…what? He had no idea, but he did know he couldn't let her go this time.

Muscles protesting, he climbed to his feet and exited the hot tub to wrap her in a giant towel before she could flee again. "Let me dry you off and you can borrow a shirt. Stop being difficult and relax."

She stood still while he swiped her radiant skin with the terry cloth, but contrary to what he'd expected, she didn't avert her eyes. Oh no, she watched him unashamedly, gaze fastened squarely on the erection he couldn't hide.

He should have gotten dressed first, obviously, if he really meant to have a drink, but this was one test of wills he did not intend to lose.

Finally, he got her dry and clad in one of his white button-downs, which did not decrease her attractiveness quotient in the slightest. But he bit his tongue, donned his own clothes and poured her a glass of wine.

One glance at his phone was enough—twenty text messages and an ungodly number of emails. Pointedly, he switched it off. What could ten more minutes of being incommunicado hurt?

She swallowed a hefty third of her wine as if intending to set the record for fastest drink between lovers.

Or she was trying to dull her senses to make it easier to spend time with him?

"I don't know how to do this," she blurted out before he'd even gotten comfortably settled next to her on the love seat.

He contemplated whether he should pretend to misunderstand or deflect with a joke. The climate felt precarious, as if he'd frighten her away if he messed up and said the wrong thing. "If it makes you feel better, I'm not sure either."

Nothing about this rekindled affair felt the same as it had the first time. Or as he'd expected it to be the second time. He'd spent his adulthood fending off money-grubbing women who cared only about the lavish lifestyle he could provide them, and somewhere along the way forgot that some people actually got something out of relationships. Companionship, maybe.

"Why does it have to be so hard?" Her fingers gripped the stem of her wineglass in what looked like a fair attempt to break it in half. "I can't find the middle ground. This is supposed to be an unemotional pleasure romp, right?"

Something rasped in her voice, a hint of sentiment that pinged inside him strangely. "You mean it's not?"

Say no. Please say something that can help me make sense of all this.

She met his gaze unflinchingly, and he couldn't break eye contact. Didn't want to. God, why was she so heartbreakingly beautiful in his shirt and with her damp hair?

"No," she whispered. "I'm afraid I'm not one of those girls who can love 'em and leave 'em."

"Well, that's easily fixed." He laughed, a little awed at how tender it came out. He wouldn't call *tender* a particular skill of his. "Don't leave."

Now, how hard was that? He should have opened with it.

"Actually, I was thinking about axing the 'love' part."

Keith went cold and then hot. No, that was definitely ice sliding down his spine. *That* was why he hadn't bared his soul from the outset. None of this had a handy spreadsheet for reference or a concrete result set.

"Now, that would be a downright shame. Reconsider."

When he picked up her hand and held it between his, she didn't pull away this time, and he greedily latched on to the small sign that he hadn't irrevocably messed up yet.

"What would you have me do, Keith?" she implored him. "I'm trying to stick to the rules, but it turns out I can't sleep with you and then forget about you the rest of the day."

She thought about him? That pleased him enormously. "I don't see what's wrong with that."

Misery tugged her mouth downward, and that hurt in a whole different way.

"I got some news today. Really good news. I wanted to share it with you."

The long pause stretched.

"But you didn't," he prompted and started to get an inkling of what was troubling her. "Is that what this is all about? You're afraid I'll feel like you're pressuring me if you tell me personal things?"

In the course of fending off women he felt nothing for other than a mild sense of affection, he'd also forgotten that relationships were about giving another person something, too. A warm shoulder. Support. Encouragement.

If he could do that with anyone, it would be with this new Cara who no longer wanted to be Mrs. Someone. The aspiring trophy wife of two years ago had completely vanished.

The thought of being there for her beyond the expo wasn't as scary as he might have supposed. Still no pressure or wedding bells. But *something*. They could define it as they went along.

"It wasn't even personal news. It was about my design business."

This was like pulling teeth without anesthesia, and he'd lost track of whom it was hurting the most.

"Cara, look at me." When she complied, eyes swimming with unshed tears, it was more like a full-on evisceration than a simple tooth extraction. "I want you to talk to me. I'm the one who asked you to stay. I'm the one who wants—"

"You're not listening to me!" And then she did yank her hand from his, tears running angrily down her face. "*I'm* the one feeling pressured. I don't want to stay. *Me.* I don't know how to do this because it's confusing. Sex and intimacy and emotions are all tied together, and what we're doing makes me think I want a relationship. I start to believe in the possibilities. And then I remember."

She remembered that I said no permanent relationship. The blank wasn't difficult to fill.

Lost in her own thoughts, she stared into the empty wineglass cupped in her palms and the silence convicted him.

"I'm sorry."

It was the most freely given apology he'd ever uttered. Because he'd pushed her into a type of relationship she couldn't handle out of pure selfishness. For once, he needed to get his head out of his rear end and pay attention to what this amazing woman wanted from him. Regardless of how uncomfortable it was.

"I know. You already apologized and I'm over it. But it doesn't make everything go away. There are still consequences."

He shook his head. "I already apologized?"

"For leaving me. But that's what it always comes down to. I start to believe and then I remember. I can't trust you."

The bomb exploded in his midsection with a sickening squelch. None of this was about the parameters of their current relationship or lack thereof but about the sins of the past. Sins he couldn't absolve. It was a target he'd missed two years ago and couldn't reverse time to correct.

Where did that leave them?

Ten

Cara shivered and nearly fell off the love seat in shock when Keith crossed to a wicker chest in the corner to retrieve a blanket. Without a word, he covered her with the navy chenille throw and returned to his seat next to her, but with a pointed foot of couch between them.

Contemplatively, he watched her. "What can I do, Cara?"

His voice washed through her, settling some of the swirl this impossible, ridiculous conversation had churned up. "There's nothing to do. It doesn't matter. We were never going to see each other again after the expo. Why does any of this change that?"

"It's not right to leave things this way."

Of course he hadn't argued the point about whether they'd see each other again.

"Because you can't stand to lose the bed-buddy benefits?" she shot back.

Ha. They hadn't made it anywhere near the bed. By design. It had become symbolic for her. No bed equaled no relationship.

"Because I hurt you," he responded quietly.

Sighing, she tucked her feet up under the blanket, but it didn't provide nearly the barrier she needed against the tension she'd foolishly introduced first by staying, and second, by not keeping her stupid mouth shut. She should have downed a glass of Keith's expensive wine and kissed him goodbye fifteen minutes ago, as she'd planned.

"Yeah. Well, there's no way around that. That's the point. I forgave you for hurting me, but I can't forget. Then you come around and you're all strong and gorgeous and telling me you see me as a success and that I'm sexier for it. We make love and I *do* forget. I hate it."

"So, here's a thought. You're not really over it," he suggested and threaded his fingers through her hair to stroke her temple, as if they were a couple who touched each other affectionately. "Let's work on that."

Together? She glanced at him, too surprised by the offer to even address the affectionate part. "What, like it's a project?"

"It's a problem. This is how I deal with problems. Head-on."

The smirk popped onto her face before she could stop it. "Not always. In my experience, you take off. It's easier to not deal with it."

To his credit, he waited without comment for her to fully process what had automatically come out of her mouth. The silence stretched, deafening her, and she had to fill it. "Okay, yeah. I get it. You're here now and that was a long time ago."

When had he become someone who stayed? She'd been too busy being the one to leave to notice.

"I'm here now," he repeated. "It's a do-over."

"But we can't really do it over, Keith. I've lost so much

in the last two years, things I can't get back. And right, wrong or otherwise, inside where I can't erase it, your name is all over it."

Her voice broke and she fought back the brimming anguish that seemed to bubble up from nowhere, but honestly, it was always there just behind her rib cage, lurking. Waiting for her to stop pushing it away.

God, he was right. She wasn't really over what had happened. Cara Chandler-Harris Designs had been a form of therapy and it had been a godsend, but running her own business hadn't fixed anything. Bandaged it more than anything, and ripping off the haphazardly applied strip had left a raw, gaping wound.

Stiffening, he sighed and rubbed the back of his neck. "I thought we talked about this and you agreed we were better off not getting married."

"Yes!" she snapped. "Because I can't trust you. Because you left me to deal with everything by myself. I'm thrilled we didn't get married if that's the kind of man you are."

He didn't flinch and God Almighty she didn't want to respect him for taking whatever she dished out. But it happened all the same.

"Isn't that the point of not being over it?" he asked more gently than she would have thought him capable of. "Deep down, you're still mad because I walked away from our wedding."

Is *that* what he thought she wasn't over? Agape, she stared at him for a moment, but he didn't seem to catch how very far off base he'd veered.

"Are you that dense? I lost a *baby*, Keith. My future child. Then you walked away. I was expecting to grieve together. To process, with you holding my hand and telling me everything was going to be okay."

"Cara… I…" A dark shadow passed through his expression and he clamped his lips into a thin line. Without a word, he slid his palm into hers, squeezing tight. Painfully tight, but she barely registered the pain when it couldn't compete with the ache in her chest.

He'd reached out. Finally.

Eyes closed, he sat frozen, anguish playing across his features. Speechless. Keith's silver tongue had deserted him, and it touched her more profoundly than anything else he could have done or said.

This was clearly difficult for him. But he was here and it encouraged her to go on, to spill the blackness inside that had become frighteningly real, very fast.

"The pregnancy was an accident. But I wanted that baby," she began slowly, sorting her thoughts as they came to her. "Then it was gone. Well, not really gone. They don't tell you that. Instead of going to Aruba on our honeymoon, I got to have a D & C."

"What is that?"

"It's…not something I care to relive." She shuddered and Keith pulled the blanket up higher around her shoulders with his free hand. "Look it up later if you think you can handle it."

With a small growl of warning, Keith tipped her chin up to force her to look him in the eye. "You handled it. By yourself. I'd like to think I'm at least as strong as you. Tell me. I want to know what happened."

The fire in his expression rendered her as speechless as he'd been mere moments ago. A strange flutter in her midsection scared her because it felt a bit like panic. *Panic.* If he'd morphed into a man she could lean on, who wouldn't desert her to deal with the horrors of a miscarriage aftermath by herself, did that mean she could trust him this time?

How would she know?

There was only one way to find out. "I think I need more wine for this."

Instantly, he complied, filling her glass nearly to the brim. And then he listened without interrupting as she told the unvarnished tale of the day before the wedding when she'd felt shuddery and nauseated but assumed it was nerves until the bleeding started. He didn't butt in when she mentioned how Meredith had sat with her through the interminably long wait in the doctor's office until the miscarriage was confirmed.

And then Cara described how she silently carried the knowledge that the pregnancy had terminated through the rehearsal dinner, smiling woodenly while friends and family toasted the couple, but slowly fading on the inside. Over the past two years, she'd often wondered if he'd picked up on the vibe because he'd been so quiet that night.

But in retrospect, he'd probably been dreading the ceremony and mentally preparing himself to enter into a union with a woman he didn't want to marry.

In the cold light of the current conversation, she realized he had been there for her in the simple fact of being willing to marry her. Had she failed to give him enough credit for that? It couldn't have been an easy decision to make or to carry out.

Coupled with his solid presence tonight, she just didn't know what to make of the still-present flutter that felt a lot less like panic now and more like anticipation.

Over half of her glass of wine remained, but she abbreviated the story of the day after the abandoned wedding. Some details were too much to repeat, but judging by the increased pressure on her hand and the bleakness in Keith's gaze, she'd given him enough of an idea what happened during a D & C to make the point.

When she stopped talking, Keith pulled her against his chest and held her fiercely, wordlessly. But no words were necessary to absorb the strength he'd offered her.

The cleansing meant everything to her.

* * *

Keith held Cara for as long as she let him and when she pulled away, it seemed as good a time as any to switch to scotch. Because he sorely needed something stout to blunt the seething mess in his stomach.

When he'd convinced her to stay, he'd envisioned a slow, languorous dive into the kind of lovemaking they'd thus far been unable to indulge in due to Cara's vanishing acts. That was the "more" he'd hoped for, not gut-wrenching emotional knots he had no idea how to untie.

The small bar in the corner of his suite provided a good cover for his shaking hands. Cara hadn't pulled many punches, that was for sure. On the second try, he clunked ice into the highball and splashed amber liquor over it, then took a healthy swallow.

Fortified, he turned back to Cara and leaned a hip against the bar, hoping it didn't look as if he was holding himself up.

He'd started this descent the moment he spied Cara across the room at the Dragonfly back in Houston. Now he had to see it through with no map and a broad field of quicksand in all directions.

"I don't know how to do this part either," he confessed.

Mostly because he had no idea what he was trying to hit. There were no goals, no tangible checklists or a specific solution to a particular problem. He had no skill set for relationships or any training, which was one of the many reasons he tried to avoid them.

Cara, as always, had turned that upside down. No matter what kind of parameters he put around their island fling, the emotional depths had been set up long ago and couldn't be sidestepped.

Besides, he owed her for messing up two years ago, owed her for jumping into this rekindled affair willingly and without censor, and most of all, he owed her for her unconditional forgiveness.

"I'm not sitting over here with a scorecard," she said. "I'd be the last person to tell you if you were doing it wrong."

He poured a second glass of scotch and opted to return to the couch. Cara's small smile bolstered him. Not a lot but enough. "I... Thank you for telling me about the miscarriage."

"Really?" She pursed her lips in confusion. "I can't honestly say what I was expecting your reaction to be, but that was not it."

He couldn't have said what his reaction should be either. But he had to man up and admit the truth. Or at least the part he could actually verbalize.

"I spent two years completely unaware you'd really been pregnant. And I've spent the last few days thinking about how I messed up." And working through the guilt. "I spent zero time thinking about how the miscarriage happened, what you must have gone through. I'm sorry."

Her strength astounded him. While he'd been admiring her business savvy and letting her cross his eyes with her new adventurous spirit, she'd actually been quietly amazing from the beginning. In his haste to escape the noose he'd created for himself, he'd missed it.

And in his haste to get her to stay tonight, he'd created an impossible internal quagmire. While processing her surprisingly calm recitation of the events, one thing had clearly risen to the surface—she'd been pregnant with a child. *His* child.

It had never been real before.

There in the low light of the temporary suite where he'd been staying for the duration of a temporary job, where he'd made love to a woman under the guise of a temporary affair, the baby became real—and just as temporary.

Something he could describe only as sadness filled him,

hitching his lungs. For the first time in his life, he mourned the necessity of temporary.

"It's okay." Her hand on his thigh was warm and reassuring. "You've had a lot to process. And you're here now. That means a lot to me."

Yes, he was here. But he sensed she needed so much more than his largely mute presence. How much longer would she put up with his inability to say the right words, to reach out and express his own feelings?

This had gotten far too complicated and he had no solution.

"Cara…" *I can't do this.*

The silence stretched and grew painful. He shifted uncomfortably, a little sick with the discovery that he wished he could be the man she deserved—but not only was he not, he couldn't be. Furthermore, she didn't trust him and he didn't blame her. What were they really doing here but resolving her issues so she could say goodbye with a clear conscience?

"I get that this is hard for you, Keith." Her espresso-colored eyes tracked his, carrying no condemnation, no expectation. Just understanding.

It nearly undid him.

"Do you really?" It came out all wrong, accusatory and harsh, but he couldn't have changed it, not with all the ups and downs and the ache at the back of his throat.

He looked away.

"Yes," she answered calmly. "I may not have known you very well back in Houston, but the reason for that is because you never let me in. I mean, I know that you grew up on Long Island and your dad worked on Wall Street. You went to Penn State and got a degree in international business. But those are just surface-level things by intention. It's not a mystery to me that you're the strong, silent type when it comes to intimacy."

She cupped his jaw and guided his face up to meet her gaze.

"It's okay," she repeated. "I meant what I said. You're here and that's enough. I'm not asking you to bare your soul."

Stricken, he stared at her, falling into her empathy with an ocean of relief swimming in his chest. She was giving him a pass and he was pathetically grateful enough to take it.

And then she sealed it with a soft kiss. Her lips rested on his and there was nothing but pure compassion in it.

"Come with me," she instructed and stood, holding out her hand.

He took it, thoroughly intrigued when she led him to the bedroom. There, she undressed him carefully and threw back the covers on the king-size bed he'd slept in alone since arriving in Grace Bay.

"We've got a long day tomorrow and we need to get some sleep." She patted the mattress. "Lie down."

She was putting him to bed. It nearly made him laugh, but it caught on the lump in his throat. "Yes, ma'am."

She was about to leave. Again.

The moment he slid under the sheet, she unbuttoned the borrowed shirt and dropped it to the floor. And then joined him, burrowing under the covers to snuggle up next to him, warm and comfortable.

"You're staying?" he asked needlessly, but in his surprise, thought it was worth the clarification.

"This is where you are," she explained simply and laid her head against his shoulder as if she belonged there. "I want to be with you. Turn off the lamp and stop talking."

But once it was dark, suddenly he couldn't shut off the swirl of unexpressed commotion in his head. The longer he stayed silent, the worse it grew.

"You know why I don't babble on about all my innermost thoughts, right?" he blurted out.

"You're a guy," Cara responded sleepily and kissed his throat.

Yes, but…it was a flimsy excuse and his DNA wasn't the real reason. Normally, he'd let it go at that but she'd been so accepting, so easy to be with. So forthcoming about her own struggles. Somehow it loosened his vocal cords. "It's because of my mother."

"Isn't it always?"

He laughed and the heaviness inside melted away. "Yeah. It wasn't okay to talk about how something made me feel. She would cut me off, change the subject. Mitchells don't talk to each other about anything except money. It's what makes the Mitchell world go 'round. Money is a tangible reward for your effort and it's the only thing that lasts."

According to George and Judith Mitchell, anyway.

"Is that how you feel about money, too?"

"Money is a by-product of success. I like the things it buys but I get more satisfaction out of seeing what I've done with this property than seeing my bank balance grow. That's the difference between my father and me. His success was measured in zeroes. It was almost like play money to him. So what if he lost a million or so dollars of a customer's money? He got a commission regardless." Unrepentant anger swept up from Keith's gut to inflame his chest. "He was so furious I didn't want to follow in his footsteps. But I didn't want money to rule me."

And he didn't want a trophy wife either, one who cared only about money, cared only about Keith's ability to earn it. Like his mother. If Keith decided to chuck it all to go live in a fishing village in the Philippines, he could and no grasping, money-grubbing woman would ever stand in his way.

In talking this through, he got the one thing he'd always

wanted from his mother but never received—someone to simply listen to him. His arms tightened around Cara and she slipped one sexy leg between his, but instead of feeling like an invitation to physical intimacy, it was all about growing closer emotionally.

He kissed her forehead. "That was probably more than you wanted to know."

"On the contrary," she corrected softly, "it was exactly what I wanted to know. I like you, Keith Mitchell. Now that I've glimpsed who you really are inside."

His lips curled up in a genuine gratified smile. She'd gotten him to share without intruding into an area he wasn't comfortable with. It was nice. "I like you, too."

Drifting in the silence, he blessed the storm that had brought them together.

The morning dawned through the floor-to-ceiling glass, nearly blinding Keith. So he shut his eyes and held the sleeping woman still tangled around him as if she couldn't get close enough.

Her firm breasts were pressed against his side, nipples rubbing his skin with every breath he took. And the more they rubbed, the faster his lungs pumped. Last night had been about something other than sex, and that had been great. A totally different experience from any he'd ever had with a woman.

But this morning, all bets were off.

They were in bed—naked—and he wanted to connect with Cara more than he wanted his heart to beat. She'd unlocked all sorts of raw, primal emotions inside and he wanted to grab on to them, before they faded.

Nudging her legs apart, he slid his thigh between them, tight against her sex. He tipped up her chin and kissed her awake. She arched against him languidly and kissed him back, slow and deep.

He was so hot and hard and ready for her, he couldn't wait. Poised at the entrance to heaven, he groaned, savoring the sensations, contemplating how slow he could reasonably take this before he came apart.

Suddenly, she broke the kiss and angled her body away from his. "Condom," she murmured.

The reminder shocked him. How could he have almost forgotten? Hadn't they both gone through enough anguish from the first pregnancy? They didn't need another one.

So why was he thinking about what it might be like if they weren't worried about an accidental pregnancy? If they had the kind of relationship where birth control wasn't a consideration?

What was he *doing* to himself? That was crazy talk, and a little misplaced sadness that nothing in his life lasted longer than a few weeks was not a good enough reason to go off the deep end.

He fumbled around on the nightstand until he found a foil packet and rolled on the barrier quickly. Satisfied, she wiggled back into place and made short work of setting off fireworks behind his eyes.

As he sank into her, spiraling into oblivion, the rawness inside blossomed into something huge and real and so perfect, there should be a whole aisle at the greeting card store devoted to it.

He just wished he knew what the aisle would be labeled. Happy Temporary Fling Day didn't have the right ring.

Finally, they heaved from bed at half past seven, a good hour later than he should have gotten up. But he wouldn't have missed that round of good-morning sex for any price. Saucily, Cara paraded around in his unbuttoned shirt and he almost blurted out an invitation to take a real vacation with him after the expo—with limited luggage, a lot of water and no cell phone.

But he didn't. If things went well, they'd both be very busy very shortly.

Before he lost his mind, he shooed her out the door with a kiss and a heartfelt "See you later." She took half a step and his hand shot out to snag hers before she could fully leave. "Stay with me again tonight."

Surprise danced around in her expression but she nodded. "Okay."

Her concession gave him perma-grin. She'd stayed last night and it had ended up being unexpectedly amazing. Maybe he could do "more" after all. Maybe they both could.

Checking his text messages wiped the smile from his face in an instant. Elena had sent him a list of items that needed attention before nine o'clock, the witching hour. Regent executives would be arriving from the airport on the dot and the resort was not ready for prime time.

While he'd been lost in his little bubble with Cara, the show had come to a screeching halt. For crying out loud. Was he the only one around here who could make decisions?

Cursing, he stabbed Elena's number and when she answered, he barked, "Talk to me."

"Where have you been?" she demanded. "I sent you like ten emails and normally you respond within a few minutes. It's like you dropped off the face of the earth."

Close. He'd dropped off the face of the resort and it was unacceptable to have left things hanging. This was his job, his reason for being in Grace Bay. Cara wasn't.

"Give me fifteen minutes and I'll meet you in the lobby. Bring able bodies and sharp minds."

Keith threw himself in the shower and scrubbed all traces of hot tubs, hot honey brunettes and intimacy from his body. He wished he could say the same about his head. Because Cara was firmly in it and no admonishment in existence could remove the memories from his mind.

He crossed the Regent emblem in the lobby in thirteen minutes.

Elena, dressed in a crisp Regent uniform, hair smoothed into a bun, waited by the front desk. Staff buzzed around the lobby, similarly dressed, attending to various duties with a heightened sense of urgency.

Regent Resorts at Grace Bay was open for business.

Keith dived in. Instead of diminishing, the list of problems grew exponentially as he began investigating.

"Pool furniture." He pointed at two uniforms. "Spread it out and make it look like we didn't lose so many pieces in the storm."

They scurried off. Keith grabbed a handful of groundskeepers. "Retrim the palm trees. They still look like they were hit by a tropical storm."

Elena rolled her eyes. "I think the executives are going to have to understand the property *was* just hit by a tropical storm."

"No. They will understand this is the premier wedding destination resort on the planet and tropical storms do not interfere with an engaged couple's plans when they stay at a Regent property."

Keith Mitchell might not control the weather but he controlled his destiny, and it was not going down in flames because he'd stumbled and fallen into the eye of Cara's whirlwind.

He sent the resort's limo to the airport to retrieve the executives and put the fear of God into the rest of the staff. True to his nickname, Mitchell the Missile's heat-seeking radar found even the smallest unearthed issues and addressed them. A general on the battlefield couldn't hold a candle to Keith's natural skill with both organization and delegation.

When the limo rolled to the curb with the executive team inside, the resort was not in the shape it should have been.

But it would be. Better the executive team see the mended seams instead of the expo guests, who would begin arriving at noon.

Keith had three hours to pull off a miracle—and convince Regent's executives to continue their faith in his ability to turn around this disaster in the making. Adrenaline pumped through his body, fueling his blood and making it sing. This was his hour of glory and he'd worked fiendishly for months to earn it.

Ronald Schmidt, the CEO of Regent, emerged first, hand outstretched for Keith to shake.

"Welcome," Keith said to the team at large and spent the next hour as a personal tour guide to Regent's entire C-suite. Simultaneously, he fielded messages from Alice and Elena and responded with a barrage of instructions as they flawlessly walked on water in Keith's stead.

At the end of the tour, Ronald shook his head with a small smile. "I don't know how you did it, Mitchell. This place is indeed the jewel you insisted it could be, even with the added complication of an unanticipated storm. Your reputation is well-founded."

"Thank you, sir." Keith inclined his head and slipped a hand in his pocket to still his yet-again vibrating phone. Interruptions could wait for a couple of minutes, especially if Ronald had more to say.

"I was going to wait until after the expo to discuss the terms of your contract, but it's clear I don't need to. As you know, the continuation clause was contingent on how you performed with this property."

"Yes, I'm aware." Tingling at the base of Keith's spine swept upward and he clamped down on it. This was no time to let euphoria interfere with what might quickly turn into a negotiation over Keith's future.

"You'll have a contract extension in your inbox within two days for the remaining fifteen Caribbean resorts. And let's bump up your rate. A million a property. We can discuss specifics whenever you're ready."

Ronald shook Keith's hand and waved to include the rest of the team. "We're all looking forward to the expo. I'm sure it will be a grand show."

"Unparalleled. I hope you enjoy your stay with Regent Resorts at Grace Bay." Keith motioned to the bellboys standing at attention behind him. "Let us show you to your rooms."

Yet another mark of distinction—treating the men who signed the paycheck of every employee here like guests. The service philosophies Keith and Elena had infused into the staff culture would catapult Regent to the top of the luxury vacation heap.

And Keith had just been granted the opportunity to do it again—fifteen more times.

It was everything he'd dreamed of when he went into consulting. It was the perfect culmination of his effort to make it on his own over the past decade. The perfect job. He could do his thing and move on; no roots, no relationships with employees…or anyone else.

Temporary ruled his life for a reason. It was what he did best. He didn't know how to do anything *but* temporary. He yearned for the next challenge, the next job that would take him someplace new, and balked at the kind of "more" Cara deserved. What could a man like that really offer her?

Nothing. He couldn't ask her to take an extended vacation. Or even a short one. He couldn't be there for her as she needed, emotionally or physically. And he hadn't even been very good at it in the first place, despite the pass she'd given him. If he'd had more practice at developing relationships, or even the skill set to try, that would be one thing. But he preferred being alone because it was easier than figuring out how to tap into an emotional center he probably couldn't ever reach.

It was a good thing he'd planned for their liaison to be finite from the beginning.

A good thing, he repeated, and wished it actually felt that way.

Eleven

Cara watched frisky sandpipers chase each other on the beach and smiled when the lead bird let herself be caught. It was worth it sometimes to slow down long enough to notice something unexpected and wonderful in the one chasing you.

Keith had revealed some pretty spectacular depths over the past few days, climaxing in the midnight soul-baring conversation. She'd had no idea he was capable of such understanding and strength—and maybe he hadn't been the first time. But he certainly was now.

Maybe the events of two years ago, and everything since, needed to happen in order to get them both to a better place. Which wasn't necessarily together. This was supposed to be a burn-off-the-excess-heat fling in the background of their real lives. The expo should be the most significant thing on *both* their minds.

Unfortunately, it wasn't, at least not in her case.

Turning her gaze back to the statuesque models in white

parading down the makeshift runaway, Cara nodded in response to Meredith's question, though she hadn't actually
heard it. The original canvas tent pavilion had been dis-
mantled in advance of Tropical Storm Mark, but unfortunately it had been stored in a nonwaterproof shed. It had
suffered severe water damage, forcing the fashion show to
take place on the beach.

As long as tomorrow's weather mirrored the calm, balmy
conditions of today, the show would still be the centerpiece
of the expo.

Meredith noted something on her legal pad and shot
Cara a smirk. "Do me a favor and smack me if I ever walk
around with such a dreamy smile on my face."

"That'll never happen," Cara promised without missing
a beat. "Because only Keith could produce such a smile and
you can't have him."

Her sister lifted a brow. "Oh my. I thought you were all
dopey-faced over the meeting with the Ever After guy and
planned to rib you about it mercilessly. But this is a much
more fun development."

The meeting with Nick Anderson was slated for tomorrow, after the fashion show, and if all went according to
plan, her design business would leap ahead of everything
she'd ever hoped for. It *should* have been the reason for a
dopey smile. Not that she was agreeing there was anything
dopey about her expression.

Cara's cheeks heated. "Shut up. You're the one who encouraged me to get Keith naked. What did you think was
going to happen?"

"I thought you were going to achieve some much-needed
stress relief." Meredith yelled at one of the models to watch
her train and tilted her head toward Cara as if about to impart a secret. "Maybe some closure. I did not think you
were going to fall head over heels again for he-who-must-
not-be-named."

"Head over heels is a bit of an overstatement." Wasn't it? Just because she'd slept in his bed didn't mean she'd gone off the deep end and started imagining a future where none existed. "He's different this time, that's all."

She wished it was easier to articulate how she felt about Keith. If she could say it to anyone, it would be Meredith, regardless of her sister's inclination to give her grief. But the only certainty in this situation was that Keith still confused her…and she still couldn't imagine trusting him enough to put his engagement ring on her finger again. He'd done very little to regain that trust.

"I think it's you who's different," her sister commented wryly. "I still remember what you said to me after your first date with him. Do you?"

Of course she did. It had come back to haunt her often enough. "I said I was going to marry him."

A premature statement to be sure since she'd only just met him. But he'd been exactly what she wanted in a husband. Successful, handsome, attentive.

Correction. What she'd *thought* she wanted in a husband. The past two years taught her the folly in her wish list. She needed a mate with the ability to stick with her through the bumps, as well as the actual desire to be a husband. Oh, and most critical—she wanted a husband who loved her and one she loved back unquestionably.

"Yep. You were really focused on getting married. Every guy you met got the Husband Test. Your man Mitchell was the first one to pass."

That was uncomfortably true. Had she forced their relationship because of her goals instead of letting their feelings evolve naturally? Her throat tightened.

Of course she had—that's how they'd gotten engaged and almost married without really knowing each other. Or being in love. They'd *both* let the pregnancy cloud their judgment. "Yeah. What's your point?"

"You haven't said a word about getting married in two years," Meredith said quietly. "That's what's different. You seem a lot less fixated on the outcome and more into the experience of the moment. It looks really good on you and in the long run will probably be a lot better for your state of mind. That's all I meant."

Cara mulled that over the rest of the day, studiously avoiding Keith as she'd done yesterday, but for a different reason this time. Yesterday, she'd still been lying to herself about whether she thought of Keith as her lover in every sense of the word. Today she knew it was too late to stop that train—and too impossible to be near him without blurting out everything on her mind.

Her sister's revelations weighed on her heavily. Meredith thought Cara was doing the right thing by falling head over heels into Keith without worrying about whether he'd marry her or not. It was exactly what this affair was supposed to be about.

And on the surface, it was. At least as far as everyone else knew. The problem lay underneath, where Cara had discovered marriage wasn't her ultimate goal after all. She wanted that and more, far more. She wanted that man Keith had been last night when he held her hand as she talked through the difficult aftermath of the miscarriage. She wanted the man who encouraged her to take her pleasure and thought it was sexy that she ran her own business.

She wanted that man to love her. And she feared a rolling stone like Keith would never be capable of that even if she gave him twenty years to get there. This was a short affair, made possible only by these special circumstances.

When Keith texted her that night, she almost didn't go. But she'd missed him and the two brief glimpses she'd gotten of him across the property as he strode off to do some Consulting Wizard task hadn't been enough to sate her.

Plus she couldn't quite get the hot tub off her mind. She should enjoy her fling to the fullest, right?

In the end, she threw on his shirt without any underwear because she liked the feel of it against her bare skin and wore the trench coat over it. A similar look had benefited her greatly last night. But when she got to Keith's room and used the key he'd given her to let herself in, he was hunched over his laptop, an open longneck beer in his left hand as he pecked at the keyboard with his right.

He glanced up but didn't otherwise move from his spot at the table, where it appeared he'd been for some time. "I'm almost finished here. Give me a minute."

The tired smile he aimed in her direction melted the ice she'd scarcely been aware surrounded her heart.

"You look like a man in sore need of a shoulder rub," she said instead of a flirty comment designed to get him away from the computer. Which she had no doubt would have worked but wasn't what he needed.

"I'm in sore need of you, period," he muttered to his laptop screen.

She stood behind him and kneaded the knots in his neck and shoulder muscles while he read a report with multicolored graphs and pie charts.

"That feels amazing." Ditching his beer, Keith groaned and leaned into her fingers, head tipped back slightly. "I didn't know my neck hurt so bad until you started doing that."

His head rested between her breasts and his lashes fluttered closed, and it was so sexy she couldn't help herself. Screw work. "Would you like me to find out what else needs attention? I'd be happy to take inventory. And yes, I mean that exactly the way it sounds," she added in case he was too tired to connect the dots.

He chuckled and reached up to still her hands, taking them into his. Instantly, he twisted her into his lap and his mouth fused to hers before she could squeal. And then she couldn't think over the pounding of her pulse as Keith's mouth drained her of everything but pleasure.

Later, she lay draped across his bed, debating whether he'd fully recovered well enough to seduce him into round two, when he cleared his throat.

"You never told me your good news."

She rolled to face him and bent up a leg casually, as if they often hung out naked and talked.

"I didn't?" she hedged. No, she hadn't. Because the intimacy they'd fallen into last night had been about the past. Necessary to heal, but not necessary to continue their affair. They still weren't a couple who shared stuff.

"Tell me." His earnest caramel gaze latched on to hers and wouldn't let go. "Unless it makes you uncomfortable. I don't want to push you into something you're not ready for."

Her heart stumbled over a beat. *He* didn't want to push *her*?

Was it possible that she was the problem in this equation? That her confusion and refusal to trust him had somehow jeopardized whatever relationship might be possible?

No. The issues were his. He didn't want a relationship and that made it irrelevant to him that she did.

"It's nothing." She shrugged, embarrassed all of a sudden to have even mentioned it, especially since it wasn't a done deal yet. "A buyer for a small boutique in Houston contacted me about selling my dresses in their stores. It's not set in stone. We're in the opening stages of discussion."

"That's great!" His effusiveness set her back teeth on edge for some reason. "I'm proud of you. That's an amazing offer and you should have told me earlier so I could order champagne."

"Save the champagne for when I close the deal," she advised and eyed him. "What's with the overly enthusiastic support?"

"I got some good news of my own today." His expression brightened and he propped his head up on his hand. "Regent extended my contract. It was contingent on the board's assessment of this property and they were so pleased with what they saw today, they offered the extension on the spot. It's two years and fifteen more Caribbean properties."

"That's...great," she said in an unintentional echo of his sentiment. But her chest had slowly frozen over as his meaning sank in and she couldn't come up with anything better.

He nodded, oblivious to her turmoil. "It's what I've been working toward my entire professional life. To show I've made it on my own merits. This is the pinnacle."

Two years. Fifteen properties. She didn't have to be a math genius to put two and two together. Keith wasn't coming back to Houston after the expo. He'd be working his magic on other Regent resorts as he'd done with Grace Bay. And she'd seen enough of his daily responsibilities to fully understand her place in his bed had come about only because of the storm. Without the lull in activity, he'd probably have continued to be too busy to make a move in her direction.

It took every ounce of her upbringing to smile and kiss his cheek. "I'm happy for you. Seems like we're both getting what we've always wanted."

It was a lie—she wanted Keith. Of course she did. All the dodging and convincing herself otherwise, all of it was a lie. And now every last shred of hope she might have gathered at the corners of her heart had been lost.

She'd tried to convince herself Cara Chandler-Harris Designs was enough. It was a business she'd built without her father's money, without any man's help, and it was hers. But it wasn't a substitute for the love of a man, a life partner she could share all the ups and downs with. It wasn't a business she'd built to get over Keith because there hadn't been anything to get over other than disappointment that he hadn't fallen in line with her fierce determination to get married.

And she knew for sure she hadn't been in love with him before because she absolutely was now and there was no comparison.

She wanted Keith but he didn't want her. There was no worse sound in Keith's mind than the clang of wedding bells.

The ache in her heart hurt in a massively different way than it had two years ago. Because she had to let Keith go instead of holding on to him to achieve her own selfish goals.

She'd gotten her wish. This was what being in love with Keith was like and it was the harshest lesson of all—sometimes love felt an awful lot like sacrifice.

Keith cleared his dry throat. He was oversharing again. He felt it in the chaste, emotionless kiss to the cheek she'd bestowed on him, could feel it in her posture, in the atmosphere.

It had started the moment he began talking. She'd slowly withdrawn, as if she wasn't really on board with staying overnight and wished he'd shut up so she could leave, even though she'd agreed this morning to stay.

Why had she said yes if she didn't want to? Disappointment lodged in his esophagus and he couldn't swallow it away. He'd been looking forward to seeing her all day. They'd have some downtime, just the two of them, when he could really savor the professional coup he'd scored today.

He'd been entertaining the notion of asking her if she'd come with him. Just to the next assignment. Just for a couple of days. A week, tops. She could sew some dresses during the day and be waiting when he returned to their room at night. No anxiety-filled, interminably long minutes as he waited for her to respond—or not—to his text message at the end of a stressful day. She'd just be there.

A sharp pull in his chest was bittersweet and he feared he'd fallen into a hole he'd never climb out of. The way he felt about Cara…it wasn't going to go away. It wasn't a slight sense of affection as he'd had the first time. This was something else, something powerful. It might be this elusive thing called love that neither of them could define.

Whatever it was, he was screwing it up.

Stupid to think she'd magically gotten over feeling pressured. The only way that would happen was if he *stopped pressuring* her.

"So why does it sound like you're the opposite of happy?" *Way to drop it, Mitchell.* Obviously he couldn't let it ride.

"I'm…tired. That's all."

So tired she couldn't muster the energy to be a little more inventive with her excuses? "Is it really so difficult to spend time with me that you'd rather be anywhere else but here?"

Her gaze snapped to his. "I wouldn't be here if I didn't want to be."

Frustrated, he vised his pounding temples between his thumb and middle finger. There was no set procedure for this conversation, but he wanted to get the best results. So he kept trying. "Then what's wrong? This contract is a big deal to me. I hoped you'd be a little more…congratulatory."

"Congratulations, Keith. It's an amazing accomplishment." She said it so sincerely, he did a double take.

"Uh, thanks. Why does it feel like I'm in the middle of a fight and you forgot to show up?"

She laughed but it rang a little hollow, ratcheting up the tension. "Because this is not a fight. We're not a couple. Therefore there's nothing to get upset over."

Fine lines around her taut mouth betrayed it as the lie he knew it was. Because he was upset too but he had no idea why. He'd like to chalk it up to stress over the expo, but it was bigger than that. They were having *some* kind of relationship. One that had evolved into something he barely knew what to do with, but that didn't make it any less real.

"What am I missing here, Cara? Saying we're not a couple is equivalent to reeling in a sea bass and then claiming you weren't fishing. Why is your line in the water if you're not trying to catch a fish?"

"God Almighty. Seriously?" Finally, she seemed to have a little more going on under the surface than she'd let on. "My line is in the water all right and it has been since we met. I've never made any secret out of the fact that I want to get married and it's also not a mystery why I'd never walk down the aisle again with *you*. Since you like fishing metaphors so much, here's mine. I'm throwing you back, sugar. Swim away and watch out for those hooks next time."

"Is this still about you not trusting me?" He rolled to his stomach, suddenly feeling exposed. "What else do I have to do? I've apologized. I've listened. I've put my mouth on your—"

"Don't be crass. This is not about trust. You can't have it both ways, Keith. Either you're in this to marry me or it's temporary. Which is it?"

A weight dropped onto his shoulders, pushing him down further with each passing moment. Who was pressuring whom here? "Who said it had to be one or the other? I thought we were having a grown-up relationship, where we enjoyed each other's company and focused on our careers."

He was losing his grip, losing his mind. Why had he tried to do this when he was so ill-equipped?

"What's that supposed to mean?" Her voice shook slightly. "Grown-ups don't want a ring on their finger?"

"No, only women who can't earn their own way. Who can't stand to be alone. I thought you were different."

It had all been a lie. She was still an aspiring trophy wife hiding behind a business that got her into the middle of as many weddings as possible.

The disenchantment was harsh and quick. And it hurt. How could it hurt?

She visibly shrank in on herself. "Is that what you think? That marriage is only something a woman would want if she can't be on her own? You think I want nothing more than to be an…an *appendage*?"

She was twisting his words, making him out to be the bad guy.

"I thought you were a woman who took charge. Who was my equal, strong and fiercely independent."

If any woman could have been his match, it was that Cara. He'd wanted more with that Cara, thought he might have figured out how to be what that Cara needed.

But she'd vanished inside an immature girl who still dreamed of being Mrs. Someone, instead of a woman who took a setback like being left at the altar and turned it into a successful business. A woman with strength and determination could handle someone like Keith, who was bound to mess up, bound to look for that next challenge. A woman like that could understand him.

He and Cara weren't even in the same book, let alone on the same page.

"And I thought you were a man who didn't see the value in something with only one purpose," she countered quietly, apparently still determined to pretend she wasn't as pissed off and frustrated as he was. "Like a wedding dress. Or frosting. I have more than one use. I'm good for more than just sex."

He shook his head and a half laugh escaped, though he found nothing funny about this fight that wasn't a fight because they weren't a couple. Maybe she really *wasn't* upset. Maybe she'd figured out that she didn't want "more" with him a long time ago and was perfectly fine with tossing him back once the expo was over.

He was fine with that, too. It was what he'd planned all along. Or at least it was what he'd planned before he actually got Cara into his bed. And before he'd gotten the contract extension. And before this conversation had started, during which he'd discovered Cara had no intention of continuing their relationship in any way, shape or form.

She'd mixed up everything.

And on second thought, he wasn't fine with any of it.

"But that's exactly my point, Cara. I don't think of you as having only one use. When you lick off the frosting, you still have cake. You're my cake, or at least I thought you were. I want you to be cake, not a mess that needs frosting to hide all the flaws. You have substance. That's what I see in you, that's what's so attractive about you."

How could she not be upset? Didn't she see how wrong marriage was for them—for anyone who valued making their own way—but how right two independent, career-minded people could be together? That's what he wanted. Right now. With the Cara he'd met since coming to Grace Bay.

"That's precious. You want to have your cake and eat it, too." She tossed her head and flopped onto her back, apparently feeling the opposite of exposed. "These metaphors are ridiculous. For once, just say what you're feeling. Or is that too hard?"

"Cara, please." She was taunting him, hitting below the belt for some unknown reason. He'd confessed to having difficulty in expressing his emotions and she was throwing it back in his face. "I'm feeling like we're not even talking the same language. You said after the newlywed game that you didn't think you wanted a relationship. Have you changed your mind? Instead of metaphors, why don't *you* say what you really mean."

"What, like I should tell you thanks but no thanks for calling me a mess and accusing me of using frosting to cover my flaws? Because that's what I really wanted to say. Or better yet, maybe I should say I don't want to get married just so I can hide a multitude of shortcomings underneath a name change."

"Then why *do* you want to get married?"

"Because, Keith." She sat up on her haunches, so thoroughly composed he wanted to rattle her just to make sure she was still breathing. "Cake is great by itself but frosting makes it so much better. I wish you could see that."

"I've lost track of what frosting is supposed to represent." Hence the reason for all the metaphors—neither of them could seem to lay it all on the line. "It would be so much easier if you'd just flat out tell me what you want me to hear."

She nodded slowly, her face blank. "After the newlywed game, I was confused. But you've helped me figure it out. I want to get married because I'm so in love with a man, and he's so in love with me, that we both have a desperate need to share everything. A bed, a house, a life, a family. Even names."

Oddly, that sounded…not so horrifying. But before he could fully process the revelation, she smiled tremulously and one tear fell.

"And that's not going to happen with you," she concluded. "So here we are, having an island fling, no pressure, no wedding bells. Stop me if you hear something that doesn't jibe."

She wanted to get married. But not to him.

So apparently *he* was the only one with difficulty in laying it all on the line. And the only one with difficulty in the parameters of their relationship, such as it was. He'd been developing all these feelings and she…hadn't. How in the hell had that happened?

Twelve

The moment of Cara's triumph had arrived.

The wedding dress fashion show, which was the highlight of the expo, would start in seventeen minutes. Cara Chandler-Harris Designs would meet the world's elite wedding professionals with a splash, yards from the pristine beach. A balmy breeze played with the white fabric sheets hanging from metal frames, which served as a makeshift barrier to separate the audience from backstage.

Every one of the brides radiated with a *je ne sais quoi* that brought to mind romance and beauty and a touch of pageantry. Cara's eyes prickled with unshed tears. Tears meant the dresses were perfect, selected with each model's attributes in mind, altered with precision.

Or it just meant she'd fallen in love with the wrong man and it sucked.

What had she expected it to be like? Moonlight and roses and a breathtaking marriage proposal by the sea?

No, actually, she'd expected it to end exactly as it had.

Badly. Because in her heart of hearts, she'd known it was going to end. But at least she'd done the right thing and pushed him away. It certainly hadn't been hard—he'd already been halfway out the door to his next resort, gleeful to turn around yet another failing wedding destination with his superhuman efforts. All the wedding and marriage talk had just been icing on the cake of his departure from her life. Like last time. Like always.

"Sand in your eye?" Meredith murmured and poked her head around the sheet to survey the audience.

"I'm fine." When Cara returned to their room last night, dry-eyed and numb, her sister hadn't so much as lifted an eyebrow, and hadn't asked any pointed questions. For that, Cara couldn't begin to express her gratitude.

It was the only reason she'd spilled everything to her sister. Every last horrible detail.

"That's good. But if you can't do this, no one would notice the hole in the lineup." Meredith nodded at Cara's dress, her gaze chock-full of sympathy. "We have five other designs to show. It's enough."

How did her sister always know the right thing to say?

"Bless you, honey. But Mulan is the first dress I designed because I wanted to, not because I had an order. It's my best work." She bit her lip and struggled not to take the easy out. "I need to wear it and I need to participate in my own show. People will love it."

More therapy. Obviously she required a lot. But she had a burning need to prove something to herself, and walking down a runway in a wedding dress somehow had become part of it.

Music piped through the sound system, and one by one the girls paraded down the runway, twirled, paused to a barrage of applause and returned to the backstage area. Cara went last.

Her smile was genuine.

She'd come full circle. Cara Chandler-Harris Designs had started as a way to get her through. And it would continue to provide her satisfaction and purpose. Nothing had changed, other than the fact that Cara could finally accept the truth.

She was always the bride, but never married. And that was okay.

Weddings were fun and she got to participate in the centerpiece of every one—the dress.

And before she'd come to Grace Bay, Cara had let the glamour and romance of the event itself seduce her into forgetting that "I do" wasn't the end of the wedding but the beginning of a marriage.

Flashes around the perimeter from professional cameras burst in rapid succession. Photographs. Of her dresses. These were magazine photographers and wedding bloggers capturing her designs to show to their readers. Which might lead to more customers.

At the end of the runway, she pivoted and held the pose to thunderous applause. Lord above, they were clapping for *her* dress. And *her* design. And Cara herself. It was heady and gratifying and fulfilling.

It flooded her all at once.

This is what Keith had meant by being cake. This feeling, this sense of accomplishment, this being in the essence of something she'd created from nothing. He'd encouraged her to forget about the frosting and focus on the substance underneath.

Cara Chandler-Harris Designs wasn't a business; it was an extension of Cara, a manifestation of her wedding dreams. Those dreams would live forever, caught in visions of silk and lace.

Marriage wasn't the most important thing she could do in her life.

The realization was freeing in a way she'd never expected. During this time in Grace Bay, she'd liked that Keith saw her as an equal, but she'd never quite figured out that to him, marriage meant inequality.

That was an aspect of the man she loved that she'd never known before. No wonder he'd fled from their first wedding. In a misguided way, he probably thought he was doing her a favor. And really, he had, in so many ways.

Keith's dark head rose above the crowd, catching in her peripheral vision as she walked back up the runway to the head of the stage, where the other girls stood in various poses. He hung back, arms crossed, watching her with a slightly hooded expression. But he couldn't have hidden his six-three frame, not in a crowd. Not from her.

Her heart recognized him instantly.

They'd parted last night in complete agreement—their island fling was over. He'd go his way, she'd go hers. But she seemed to be the only one unhappy about it.

After the show ended, Cara turned to follow Meredith and the other girls back to their rooms. The dresses should go back into airtight bags as soon as possible, especially because Cara had a feeling she might be selling all of them very shortly.

"Ms. Chandler-Harris?"

Cara turned to the male speaker, an elegantly dressed man in his midthirties who obviously knew his way around a stylist and wasn't afraid to be seen shopping at Bloomingdale's. His name placard read Nick Anderson—Buyer for Ever After Boutiques.

She swallowed a great big ball of sudden nerves. "Mr. Anderson. How lovely to meet you. I've spent many hours in your boutiques."

"Checking out the competition?" he asked with an innocuous smile as they shook hands.

"Daydreaming," she corrected graciously. "That's what

we both sell, right? A bride's dreams, plucked from her mind and brought to life in fabric."

Hooking arms with Mr. Anderson, she walked with him along the beach and spun the tale of a woman who loved being a bride so much, she'd created wedding dress after wedding dress to celebrate that bright, brief moment when all eyes were on the most beautiful woman in the room.

And when it was Nick Anderson's turn to talk, he smiled. "You've hooked me. What will it take to get your designs in my stores?"

"Well, my stars. You flatter me," Cara drawled to cover the hitch in her throat. And she only wished it was because she'd just been handed a golden opportunity.

But that was secondary to the intense desire to leap into Keith's embrace and tell him she'd done it. She wanted him to kiss her and say how proud he was.

Instead, she smiled through the twinge pulling at her heart. "Let's get down to business, shall we, Mr. Anderson?"

Keith watched Cara stroll off with a man entirely too well put together to be trusted. And she was still wearing her long white dress. It was the same one she'd been wearing that first day, when he'd accosted her in the pavilion during the fashion show run-through—on purpose because he'd wanted to catch her off guard.

Of course, he'd been the one flattened.

She'd been just as stunning then as she was now and always had been. The white dress with the high collar and clean lines only heightened her lush beauty, as if she'd been born to wear that exact dress as she walked down the aisle toward a besotted groom. They'd promise to love each other forever and the poor dimwit would whisk her away to a honeymoon at a resort like this one, where they'd hardly venture out of their suite because they were too wrapped up in each other.

Maybe her groom wouldn't be this too-carefully dressed expo guest, but she'd marry someone eventually.

Jealousy—big, green and ugly—flared in Keith's gut, and he did not care for it any more than the sharp longing and utter confusion Cara had provoked the moment she'd stepped out on that stage.

"Still got my eyes on you, Mitchell."

Keith whirled. Meredith stood behind him, tapping one stiletto against the sand, which should have been impossible but the laws of physics apparently didn't apply in the Chandler-Harris world.

"Great," he growled. "You can watch me get back to work."

The mock wedding was scheduled to round out the day's events, and the crew still needed to tear down the runway from the fashion show before the chairs could be set up. A sunset wedding starring a couple of actors would put the cherry on top of the resort's launch.

Without Cara's help, he had a suspicion it wouldn't go as well as the run-through. Mary would do her best but the resort still hadn't hired a full-time wedding coordinator.

Thoughtfully, he eyed Meredith. "Since you apparently have nothing better to do than hang out with me, how about giving me a hand?"

"Are you out of your mind?" She laughed. "I wouldn't help you if you were the last man on earth. Besides, I have a strict policy that I only help men who can repay me with sex, and I have a feeling that wouldn't go over so well."

"I'm pretty sure Cara wouldn't mind," he shot back without thinking and then cursed.

He might as well have come right out and admitted she'd messed him up. That he'd lain awake last night for hours trying to understand why he'd gotten exactly what he'd asked for—a short-lived affair, no pressure, no wedding bells—and he was miserable.

Not only was he miserable, Cara had already moved on, apparently, to someone who made her laugh as they strolled on the beach, arm in arm. So why would Cara care whom he slept with, even if it was her sister?

He never should have let even that much slip. This wasn't a random drive-by. Meredith wanted something and she was smarter than nearly everyone gave her credit for. He'd never figured out why she hid it behind overblown sex appeal.

"Oh, I'm pretty sure she would mind. But I have a feeling you'd mind even more. Why are you standing here talking to me instead of going after her, anyway?" Meredith hit her head with the heel of her hand as if she'd just remembered something important. "That's right, you're an idiot."

"Thanks, I appreciate your assessment," he commented drily. "Is this your way of buttering me up before you get to the real point of this ambush?"

Meredith flashed him a smug grin. "Don't tell Cara, but I've always liked you. For her, I mean. You'd drive me to homicide in under four seconds flat."

"The feeling is mutual." God help the man who fell in love with Meredith. He'd have to be made of sterner stuff than Keith.

Thankfully, he'd picked the right sister from the start. Cara was the only woman he'd ever considered an equal, the only woman capable of getting him to talk about his feelings—however brief of a discussion that had ended up being. The only woman who'd ever triggered such strange rawness in his chest.

And she was the only woman he'd ever tried to be there for when she needed him. Fat lot of appreciation he'd gotten for that.

"Since we agree we wouldn't touch each other with a

ten-foot pole, how about you stop being such a weenie about the woman you do want? Please tell me you're not going to mess it up with Cara *again*."

"You should be reading the riot act to your sister. *I'm* not the one messing it up." They'd had something perfectly fine that worked for both of them. Why couldn't their relationship continue as is, no pressure, just two people who liked spending time together? Cara's insistence on being Mrs. Mitchell or nothing had ruined it all. Ruined the fledging feelings that Keith could barely admit to himself, let alone to her.

"You're impossible. How do you think I know that's not true? I *did* talk to Cara. She let you go because she didn't want to force you into another unwanted trip down the aisle."

He snorted unevenly, guilt crowding into his lungs. "Cara couldn't have done that at gunpoint."

"Exactly. And given what happened the first time, can you blame her for not wanting to introduce any more *accidents* into the mix?" Meredith's laser-sharp gaze tore through his flesh to pierce his heart. "She gave you up, despite being madly in love with you, because she didn't want to unintentionally trap you into marriage. Happy with yourself, Mitchell?"

Keith's knees turned to jelly. "She's in love with me? Why didn't she say anything?"

The notion planted itself in his chest and spread. Cara was in love with him. For real, this time. She wouldn't have told Meredith if it wasn't true.

Meredith shook her head with a grunt of disgust. "I take it back. I don't like you. You're a moron and Cara can do much better. You deserve to spend the rest of your life alone. Good luck with that."

Mahogany hair flying, Meredith turned her back on

Keith and stomped off through a sea of wedding professionals socializing on the beach.

Keith's gaze lit on Cara and her friend as they stood talking near the shoreline. Their faces fuzzed under his scrutiny and his own face superimposed itself over that of the man standing by the woman Keith had held in his arms last night. The woman he'd walked away from once again because he couldn't do what she wanted.

No, he'd refused to do what she wanted. Refused to even consider the possibility that marriage could be something other than a cold union designed to give a woman a life of luxury. Maybe it was like that with some people. Maybe it would have been that way with the Cara he'd almost married the first time.

But everything was different now. *She* was different. And he'd skipped right over the possibility that marriage could be something else. Cara had never even given him a chance to figure out what their relationship could be, just waltzed out the door and didn't even bother to tell him something so important as the fact that she'd fallen in love with him.

And hearing it from Meredith instead of Cara was unacceptable. She owed him an explanation for how she'd figured out something so monumental.

Suddenly he had a perverse need to hear it from Cara's own lips.

"Mr. Mitchell." One of the groundskeepers launched into a question about the mock wedding setup that Keith barely heard.

"Excuse me." Keith stepped around the uniformed man, leaving him hanging midsentence, and strode across the sand with nary a thought for his best Italian shoes.

He crashed Cara's little party with the same amount of remorse—none.

"Keith Mitchell." He stuck his hand out and sized up the

man as they shook. He was too pretty, too well dressed and too short for Cara.

And their conversation was over.

"Come with me, Cara," Keith said shortly and drank in the luminous vision in white, so beautiful, his lungs hitched.

"I'm a little busy," she responded just as shortly. "Can't it wait?"

No. It couldn't. And he was this close to picking her up and throwing her over his shoulder to take her somewhere private so she could explain *right now* why she could tell Meredith about her feelings but not Keith. He wanted to hear her say she loved him and then he could figure out what to do about it.

That's when he actually read the guy's name tag. The word *buyer* leaped out and whacked him upside the head. This must be the source of Cara's good news. And he'd intruded like a jealous lover.

Well…he kind of was a jealous lover. And he deserved every bit of the heat in Cara's glare.

"It can wait." Keith nodded to the man who was likely offering Cara the business proposition she'd mentioned. "Sorry I intruded. Cara, text me when you're free. Meet me in my office."

"Sure. See you later," she said and shifted her gaze pointedly. *Go away.* It wasn't hard to interpret.

Morosely, Keith cooled his heels in his office for a solid thirty minutes, holding his phone like a lifeline, shaking it occasionally. Still no text messages.

But he did get three phone calls from Mary asking his opinion about the mock wedding setup and all Keith could tell her was to use her best judgment. Mary's return comment summed it up.

"You should keep Cara around permanently. That woman knows brides."

She did. And she knew that she wanted to be one. Keith had bad-mouthed marriage for the past week, so of course she'd bailed on him. Yeah, he *was* a moron. Cara hadn't told him she'd fallen in love because he hadn't given her any reason to.

Just as he hadn't given her any reason to meet him in his office. She wasn't coming. And he couldn't blame her.

If he hoped to salvage anything from this debacle he'd made of their relationship, he needed to go big or go home. It was time to turn around the one thing he'd resisted thus far—himself. Mitchell the Missile had a very worthy target to hit.

And if he wanted to hear from Cara's lips that she loved him, he probably needed to admit he'd fallen in love with her, too. Out loud. To her.

The revelation would probably shock her as much as it had shocked him.

Cara perched on the white wooden folding chair in the first row, where the groom's family would normally sit if this were a real wedding. But since the bride and groom were actually actors Mary had hired to perform for the expo guests, Cara didn't think anyone would mind if she grabbed a good seat.

She loved weddings. No doubt about it.

Her island fling with Keith had given her back the ability to see a wedding for what it was—a celebration of love and commitment between two people who wanted to be together. She'd never settle for anything less and if it meant she'd never experience a walk down the aisle, that was the price of holding out for love.

Still clad in Mulan, Cara carefully crossed her legs so she wouldn't rip a seam. She should have gone back to her room and changed, but she couldn't bear to take it off yet. The dress had become symbolic of the growth in Cara

Chandler-Harris Designs, of her own growth. And it was her dress and she liked wearing it.

Music piped through the sound system and the bride floated down the sand aisle, barefoot, exactly as Cara had suggested to Mary. When the bride reached her groom, the minister, also an actor, began the ceremony.

"Dearly beloved…" The minister droned through the first bit and then said, "If anyone objects to this union, speak now or forever hold your peace."

"I object."

Keith's voice cut through the balmy sunset atmosphere. Cara whirled and there he was, waltzing up the aisle as if he owned it. He halted at the first row, gaze on Cara.

Everyone else's gaze was on him. Yummy Interrupting Man had struck again.

"On what grounds?" the minister asked on cue, as if this was part of the script.

"On the grounds that every wedding should unite two people who are in love with each other," Keith said but not to the minister. His melty caramel eyes held fast to Cara. "The bride and groom don't qualify."

"What are you doing?" Cara whispered.

"What I should have done two years ago," he said at normal volume because obviously all the expo guests should be included in a discussion about their ill-fated history. "And last night. Instead of walking away, I'm in the middle of a wedding. Where you want me."

The power of speech nearly deserted her but she managed to keep her composure. Somehow. What was he up to?

Warily, she swept him with a bored once-over. "Well, sugar, that's mighty nice but if I recall, your Speedy Gonzales shoes make quite an impression, especially at weddings."

"That's why I took them off." He lifted one bare foot for emphasis. "I'm not going anywhere."

Her heart stumbled and erratic beats throbbed in her throat as she finally caught up. He'd interrupted the wedding to make a specific point, but he was sure taking his sweet time in getting there. "What's this all about?"

Had he crashed the mock wedding because she hadn't responded to the royal summons to his office? Unlikely. The fashion show had been her crowning achievement and this was his. Keith Mitchell had turned Regent Resorts into a premier wedding destination and the mock wedding should be the highlight of it.

Why was he ruining it?

Keith skirted the chairs and knelt by her feet. Almost as if—

No! He wasn't about to sweep her up in some sort of sham proposal strictly as part of the show. He wouldn't dare.

Then he took her hand, his gaze swimming with earnestness and something else she couldn't place, couldn't fathom, and she couldn't look away.

"I have trouble expressing myself," he said. "I like that you don't force me to dredge up what's inside. But you deserve more. I want to give you more. I want to stop pretending temporary is all I can do instead of sticking around and figuring out how to say what I'm feeling."

Sincerity resonated in every word out of his mouth. Oh, this was real. So achingly, wonderfully real.

A hum in her tummy spun outward to sweep across her skin with a delicious heat. "So temporary *isn't* all you can do?"

He shook his head. "Not anymore. I want to give you everything your heart desires. No matter what it is. Losing you is unacceptable. Because I love you."

The crowd murmured and sighed as all the blood drained from her head and white stars burst behind her eyes. "What?"

"It's for real." His voice dipped, laced with all sorts of emotions. "I'm sorry it took external forces to get me to realize it."

"Meredith told you what I said, didn't she?" Sisters. Can't live with them, can't shoot them. "That...blabbermouth."

Of course, her interfering sister's conversation with Keith had prompted all of this so maybe it wasn't so bad that Meredith couldn't keep her fat mouth shut.

Keith nodded once. "I'd like to hear it from you, though. That's what I wanted to talk to you about earlier."

Oh my. Stubbornness had nearly cost her everything. Fortunately, Keith wasn't one to sit around and wait for life to happen. She heaved a happy sigh. "Yeah, I'm afraid it's true. I do love you. But I can't believe that's what it took to get you on your knees."

"It didn't. When I saw you in that dress, that's when it clicked. I want to marry you and be there for you every moment of every day for the rest of our lives."

Her chest squeezed and she forgot to breathe. *Marriage.* Keith was talking about marriage. Obviously he'd been out in the sun too long. "That's crazy, Keith. It's just a dress."

"That's where you're wrong. It's special because it's *you* in the dress. Be my bride, but not just for one day. Every day."

Her heart lightened all at once. He really and truly got her. For so long, she'd yearned to wrap herself in the experience of getting married, to put on the dress as if it held some mystical power. But eventually, you had to take it off and start the marriage.

And there was no one she'd rather do it with than this man, who'd crashed a fake wedding to turn their relationship into something real, who encouraged her to be his equal, who'd told her to grab what she wanted. And she wanted Keith Mitchell.

"Cara, I want to share everything with you. Houses, names, futures. Say you'll marry me."

She held the hand of the man she'd sworn to never trust, to never let crush her again, to never be in the presence of while wearing a wedding dress. Looked as if the answer was easy.

"Yes."

Epilogue

Dawn burst through the floor-to-ceiling glass in the honeymoon suite and the pristine beach spread out in both directions as far as the eye could see. Cara snuggled up against Keith's warm body and watched the sun rise over Aruba from their bed.

"I don't think I'll ever get tired of this view," she commented. "It doesn't seem to matter that I've seen it every morning for two months straight. It never gets old."

"I agree, Mrs. Mitchell," Keith murmured, his gaze on Cara and not the panoramic scene outside their room. "You are definitely the best thing in the world to wake up to every morning."

Was it possible for your heart to actually burst from happiness? She hoped not. "Ha. That's not what you said yesterday. I believe your exact words were, 'Stop that or you'll make me late for the third day in a row.'"

Her husband laughed. "Yeah, I guess I did say that. And you did not stop if I recall."

Cara shrugged. "Sorry. That's what you get when you bring a girl to a resort in Aruba and then insist on working the whole time."

She liked to think of it as fate that the next resort on Regent's turnaround agenda was located in Aruba, the same island she and Keith had selected for their canceled honeymoon two years ago. But they'd made it to the altar, and the honeymoon, this time.

"It's my job," he said, and not the least bit apologetically. "Which you encouraged me to take right away, I'll remind you. I wanted to take some time off but you were worried Regent would amend the contract."

Yeah, that *was* her fault. The day after the expo concluded, Keith had marched Cara down the sand aisle and married her in a real wedding on the beach in Grace Bay, with no ring, no influential guests and no fanfare. But there'd been plenty of love and a desperate desire to be united in matrimony. It had been the most romantic thing that had ever happened to her.

She'd repaid him by insisting he start immediately at the next resort. Because he loved his job and she loved him. Of course, when her husband's job promised to take them to fifteen different versions of paradise over two years, it was a little hard to complain about much of anything.

"Yes, the contract. That was the reason." She kissed him soundly and shoved him out of bed. "Go to work. I'll be here later."

Keith grinned. "Be naked when I get back."

"Maybe." She pretended to contemplate but it was pretty much a sure thing. "I have to finish Yvette's dress but then I might be available."

Keith made short work of getting dressed in a delicious dark suit that she couldn't wait to strip him out of at the end of the day. "Now who's the workaholic? I thought Meredith was taking over more of the business since you're in bou-tiques and have more orders than you can handle?"

Cara had asked Meredith to be a full partner and even offered to change the name to Chandler-Harris Designs, but her sister had pointed out that she was the only Chandler-Harris around and until Meredith could afford to buy into the company, Cara's name should remain.

"She is. But the company is still mine."

"That's my bride." Keith blew her a kiss and went to ter-rorize the resort staff.

Yes, Cara was a bride…and a wife and a business owner. Instead of replacing one with another, she'd gotten it all, thanks to her perfect husband who had made her life com-plete.

* * * * *

If you loved Cara's romance,
pick up her sister Meredith's story

FROM FAKE TO FOREVER

Available now from award-winning author
Kat Cantrell
and Harlequin Desire!

If you're on Twitter,
tell us what you think of Harlequin Desire!
#harlequindesire